Buhle

To Jackie,

May this book be a constant reminder
of the "shaken but not-stirred"
meeting of the PD group.
  Your charming presence brought
  a ray of sunshine to our lives.
                Best-wishes
                Logan

                281-538-1056

This is a work of fiction. Names, characters, places and events are used fictitiously.
Any resemblance to actual events, locales, organizations or persons, living or dead is
entirely coincidental.

LOGAN NATHAN

BUHLE

2007

Buhle

The Chapters Of This Book Are Bandages That Served To Cover The Onslaughts Of An Earlier Life. I Dedicate This Book To The Women In My Life Whose Enthusiasm And Support For The Writing Of This Book, Was The Balm That Healed My Soul.

INTRODUCTION

I was tempted to introduce my book with this paragraph;

"A country ravaged and raped by the apartheid years, conceived and delivered a quadruple nation of White, Colored, Indian and Black people. Like an episiotomy, the Government regime of Whites in power, tore the country by polarizing the people into two groups; the White and Non-white populations. The development of this infant nation, under the guardianship of the apartheid regime was stunted by ignorance of each others worth. And so with this handicap, the country stumbled forward with strife and oppression tainting everyone's lives", but decided against it as it portrayed me as a hurt and angry person, and I am not that. South Africa has molded me to be humble and compassionate, and for that I am thankful. In keeping with my spirit here is my introduction:

With the arrival of the first White settlers to the Southern tip of Africa, in 1652, South Africa was ushered into an era where a person's destiny was influenced by the color of their skin. Over the next three hundred and fifty years the people of color in South Africa fought for recognition of their individual identities and ethnicity.

"Apartheid" which meant "apartness" was the word that described the policy of separate development of people of different color and ethnic backgrounds. The inequitable apartheid policy practiced by the White only minority government sparked a period of racial tension and oppression. The country was plagued by politically motivated arrests, torture and untimely deaths whilst in detention.

The Zulu people of South Africa where one of several Non-white groups that suffered under the discriminatory laws of apartheid. This fictional story is about a beautiful young Zulu girl aptly named Buhle (*Bush-le*), whose simple life was drastically changed one night, triggering a tragic chain of events that eventually led to disaster. This story celebrates the human spirit in the face of hardship and tragedy. It warms the heart to know that compassion for another human is not based on the color of one's skin or ethnic background.

CHAPTER 1

When the rustling in the sugar cane field stopped and the sugar cane stalks stopped thrashing around and when the begging and crying stopped, Rupin knew it was over. Rupin sat in the passenger front seat of the car looking through the windshield watching the water vapor of the earlier humid afternoon condense on the cool glass of this evening. A bead of water collected on the top of the windshield and rolled down the glass, leaving a wet trail behind it. The heaven above had just shed a tear for that poor innocent girl; she did not deserve what just happened to her. Rupin's thoughts returned to the sugar cane field, it was quiet now; there were no more sounds of begging.

As if in a vacuum, Rupin heard the sounds around him slowly return, dragging him out of his trance. The gentle rumble of the engine reminded him that Devraj had left the engine running when he dashed out of the car. The sounds of crickets around him reminded him that he was sitting on a deserted dirt road that cut through the middle of a sugar cane field. The headlights of the car rudely intruded into the dark void around him and the illuminated interior dome light of the car was a solitary beacon to his presence. The driver's door was ajar since Devraj in his haste did not close it when he dashed out of the car. In the subdued light, Rupin could see his reflection in the rearview mirror and it startled him. It was the first hard fact that hit him, he was physically there and although he did nothing, he was just as responsible for doing nothing.

Buhle in the Zulu language meant beauty in English and the name suited her perfectly. She was affectionately known as Buhle and everyone in her small village community they called the "umuzi" loved her warm ready smile and shy personality. Buhle Khulekani was a Zulu girl, barely eighteen years old who lived in a clustered settlement called an umuzi located at the South Coast of KwaZulu Natal in South Africa. The umuzi was nestled among the hills in rolling fields of sugar cane on the outskirts of a small town called Harding. The umuzi consisted of approximately twenty beehive-shaped huts that housed a small Zulu community. The Zulu people are the Nguni nation who descended from the tribe who migrated to the south along the east coast of South Africa and settled there. The Nguni people speak softly and smoothly and tend to be scantily clad. They are not ashamed to be naked amongst themselves with little covering at the front and back.

Buhle was blessed with a curvy figure with well-endowed breasts and shapely legs. Buhle however did not consider this to be a blessing since her sexy figure drew lusty glances and advances from the testosterone charged young males in the umuzi. What made Buhle every young male's dream was not just her physical appearance but her captivating smile and soft tender nature. Buhle wanted to fall in love, marry and raise a family. She was a simple girl with simple needs.

Like all young women in the umuzi she needed to support herself and her father after finishing her school years. Higher education at a college was not an option as she needed to take care of an aging and sick father. Her mother had passed on several years prior, having succumbed to breast cancer. To add to her responsibilities, her father was not in the best of health and could not work to support her. He relied on Buhle for his well being and Buhle was honored to care for him. She adored her father and would not have had it any other way.

Being in the late nineteen seventies, jobs for the Black South African women in the area were primarily as domestic maids for the white South African farmers. With her round face and easy smile, it was easy for Buhle to get a job as a maid at the DuPlessis residence located at their sugar cane plantation close by. She had to walk about five miles each way from her umuzi to the DuPlessis farm house, the distance reduced by her taking shortcuts through the sugar cane fields. Buhle worked long hours. She had to leave home at five in the morning to be at the farm house by six. She found that on most days she could only leave the farm house after the family had their dinner and the dinner dishes were washed and put away. This would put her on the road back home at eight in the evening. Although she got paid about ten South African Rand a week, at that time about fifteen US dollars, Buhle didn't mind this as her meals were provided at the farmer's home and the White DuPlessis family she worked for, treated her well. On some evenings she was allowed to take home some of the left over food from the dinner table. This helped her tremendously as she did not have to go home and cook dinner for her father.

Most days the walk back home at night was not bad. In fact Buhle looked forward to it. She was under a clear sky and she would skip and dance on her way home singing her favorite Zulu song. Although she lived in South Africa during apartheid times under White oppression, she did not care; she was free under these heavenly skies. She would fantasize of meeting the man of her dreams and how she would make a home for him and her four children. Her mind was a perfect playground for her dreams and she conjured up all kinds of scenarios with her fantasy family. On days that the weather was bad, especially when there were torrential rains, Annie DuPlessis, the farmer's wife, insisted that she stay overnight in the utility room that was attached to the shed outside the farmhouse. Over the months she had carved out a spot in that utility room that she called her home away from home. There was a little crawl space that she had cleaned up and used for storing her personal belongings and some clothing. When the weather was bad, her father did not expect her home and he resigned himself to eating dry bread with some watered down milk for his evening meal.

This evening was no different to most evenings; Buhle was feeling good about life. She held in her hand a piece of steak left over from the farmer's evening meal. She looked forward to seeing the look in her father's face when she served it to him. Meat was a rare luxury in Buhle's home and she knew that her father would cut the meat delicately into two pieces. One piece would be about a third in size of the whole piece of meat. Without drawing attention to the smaller piece on his plate, he would quickly place the larger piece on her plate. Before she spotted the inequity, he would put his piece of steak in his mouth and chew it with relish. Buhle would smile at this routine when it occurs and she would make a promise to herself that she would find a man to marry who was like her father.

Although it was dark she did not stumble in the dirt road. She knew every bump in that road having walked across this shortcut many times before. She never felt unsafe here since no one used this road so late in the evening. These were working class people: farmers and laborers who went to bed early so that they could make an early start the next morning. Buhle was therefore surprised when she heard the rumble of a car approaching her slowly along the dirt road. The car seem to be bouncing as it hit every bump in the road and Buhle smiled as she imagined the car's headlights bouncing in the dust like a crazed bull in a rodeo. As the car drew closer Buhle stepped aside to let it pass and in her naivety waved and smiled broadly to the occupants.

So that she did not get any dust in her eyes and nose, Buhle held her breath and closed her eyes as she waited for the car to pass. She waited until she could not hold her breath any longer. She opened her eyes as she took a long deep breath and saw the car stop along side her. She figured that these folks were lost and needed directions. She could barely make out the occupants but she was sure that they were two Indian men in the car. The apartheid system in the country separated people by the color of their skin and their lineage and thus it was common to identify strangers by their race. The interior of the car was dark and the car's headlights were blinding her and it made it difficult for her to make out their faces. This made her a little nervous as she did not like to talk to someone whose face she could not see. As she was deciding on whether or not to just keep walking or stand there, the driver's window rolled down.

"Are you lost?" Buhle inquired nervously.

"Now that we have found you sweetheart, we are no longer lost?" came a voice from the gloomy darkness of the car's interior.

Although she could speak English, Buhle did not understand the response. Still keeping her smile and clutching the piece of left over steak even more firmly in her hand, Buhle nervously asked,

"Do you need help?" The answer came back with a cackle,

"Yes we need help. We need your help. Get in the car and we can talk about it."

Still rooted to the spot, Buhle was trying to figure out what these people wanted when the driver opened his door abruptly. She was startled by the sudden movement and all her senses urged her to flee, but she could not move. As the car door opened to let Devraj, the driver out, the car's interior dome light came on and she saw Rupin's face in the dim illumination. Rupin was the passenger in the car and he had a gentle thin bony face with sad eyes. Buhle noticed the birth mark on the side of his face and a faint recognition triggered in her mind. As she looked at Rupin's face she saw it turn suddenly to surprise and then to alarm as he realized what Devraj was going to do. The change in Rupin's face triggered a flight response in her and she turned on her heels and plunged into the sugar cane field closely followed by Devraj who clawed the air behind her trying to grab her. She instinctively knew what this man wanted and she hated her body for it.

She had waited too long to flee because Devraj was only one step behind her, clawing at the back of her clothing to bring her down. The sugar cane slashed and whipped her body as she went hurtling through them and they slowed her down. Devraj had gained the advantage and like a lion attacking a deer, he launched himself at her back bringing her down. Although she had never been with a man before she knew that it would hurt. She remembered some of her school friends telling her how uncomfortable the experience was. Buhle was now sobbing and pleading for Devraj to let her go, but he was too crazed to listen. Devraj was stronger than she was and he easily grabbed her in a wrestling move and flipped her over onto her back. As her head came down it hit the side of a rock embedded in the sand. She saw a flash of white and shooting stars as she slumped over the precipice into unconsciousness.

As she slid down that slippery slope into the abyss, she was vaguely aware of her undergarments being ripped off her. She tried desperately to protect herself but her hands had already turned to mush. The last words that escaped her lips were "please stop" as she slipped into oblivion. A searing pain jolted her body and sent a spasm through her abdomen, her conscious mind never felt it but it registered in the core of her subconscious.

As Buhle emerged from the darkness into the conscious world she was vaguely aware of a rustling sound near her head. Her head and body hurt in so many places that it was just easier for her to lie there and rest. She was not fully awake and had not fully comprehended what had happened to her. She was probably unconscious for about ten minutes. The rustling sound continued and she turned her head to see where it was coming from. Her eyes focused on a large furry rodent tearing away at the tin foil that held her piece of steak. A realization came screaming back at her like a run away freight train; that rodent had her father's steak in its mouth.

She bolted upright and grabbed for the steak, but the large rodent was quicker. As it scurried away with the steak still firmly clenched in its mouth, Buhle lunged for it. Buhle would have caught it had it not been for her pants that was still around her one ankle and which had snagged on a small tree stump; it brought her down face first onto the dirt floor.

Buhle sat up sobbing and she wasn't sure whether she was sobbing for the lost steak dinner or the pain that racked her body.

She remembered that, earlier that evening, she had emptied out unfinished portions of steak from the other dinner plates into the outside garbage can. She was determined to get her father a steak dinner tonight. So hauling herself up, she pulled up her pants, grimacing with the tenderness she felt and made her way back to the farm house.

That night her father had a steak dinner; while she heated a large pot of water on an open wood fire outside her hut. She told no one of what had happened, it was going to be her dark secret to hide. She desperately needed a bath to wash away the filth that had crept inside of her. The transgression that occurred that night was buried deep into the souls of the three present at the sugar cane field. None of them ever spoke of what had happened but its curse and consequences hovered over their lives forever.

CHAPTER 2

Although her body ached all over and she needed the rest, Buhle was wide awake long before sunrise. She was thankful that it was Saturday morning and she did not have to go to work. Buhle dreaded to think of what had happened but she needed to address in her mind the previous night's event. She felt safe to visit the events of the previous night because her father was still asleep and would not be aware of the turmoil in her mind. Buhle racked her brain trying to think of when and how she had offended the AmaDlozi for her to be punished this way.

Buhle believed in Nkulunkulu, her God, the creator of mankind. But she did not pray to her God, her prayers were to the spirits of her ancestors, the AmaDlozi. When bad things happen it is usually seen as evil sorcery or the spirits were angry. Prayers and pleas to the angry spirits are usually channeled through the Sangoma who was the spiritual healer in the umuzi. The Sangoma decided on how to appease the spirits and if she decided that witchcraft was involved then a sacrifice was offered to the spirits.

Buhle decided that she needed to consult the umuzi Sangoma to help her deal with this curse. But she was afraid of the Sangoma who was a powerful figure in the umuzi. Buhle was especially concerned about the possibility of a sacrifice. Buhle decided that she needed some fresh air to think this through, so she decided to go outside her hut into the cool morning even though it was not yet daylight.

She very quietly slipped out of her simple bed so as to not disturb her father who was sleeping soundly in the other corner of the hut. Buhle put on a gown that she had sewn from cloth bags. They had bought corn powder from the local grocer in bags made of strong woven linen cloth. The crushed and ground corn power served as the staple food that provided the bulk of carbohydrates in their meals. Buhle had always thought that the only reason they bought the corn powder was for the cloth bags. With the stealth of a cat, Buhle exited the hut into the cool morning air.

Her breath came out in short puffs of vapor smoke, as she struggled to get accustomed to the cold air. She blew into her closed fists to warm her hands as she debated whether or not she should return to her warm bed. Before she could decide a pair of strong muscular arms wrapped around her breasts from her rear. Buhle sucked in the cold air to scream but stifled the scream when she heard a familiar low teasing whisper in her right ear.

"My Buhle, is cold this morning, let me warm you up" the man behind her breathed into her ear, his breath sour from the ijuba he had been drinking the night before. Ijuba is a sorghum beer, a national drink of the Zulus available at most drinking halls in the vicinity. Buhle recognized the aggressive advances of Mapoza a local umuzi Casanova who was older than her. Mapoza always lusted after Buhle, but she kept him at arms length. Mapoza wanted her but not in the same way as he wanted his other women. The other women gave themselves up willingly to him and once they fell pregnant with his baby, he moved on to a new conquest. Mapoza wanted not only Buhle's body but he wanted to conquer her mind and spirit. He wanted all of her, but he was not prepared to take it by force; he wanted her to fall in love with him.

Buhle still recovering from the night before was repulsed by a man touching her. The bile in her stomach refluxed in her throat and she wanted to throw up. The nausea that engulfed her head made her swoon and her legs buckled. Mapoza, who was not aware of what was going on, expected her to fight him off as she always did. Instead she weakened in his arms and he immediately became aroused. He saw this as a submission and it was good enough for him. He grinned from ear to ear not believing his luck as he scanned the area looking for a spot her lay her down.

A twig crackled behind a nearby tree and Mapoza looked up startled. It was not yet daylight and he was not expecting anyone to be up so early. He looked in the direction of where the sound came from and he saw a dark figure duck behind the tree trunk. The person was not fast enough as he recognized the form, it was Themba. Mapoza was angry; he resented being followed by this umuzi idiot. Themba was short for Bhekithemba and he was indeed treated by every one as the umuzi idiot. Mapoza let Buhle go and she slumped to her knees. He raised his hands in frustration and stormed off without looking back. Mapoza and

Themba were brothers, but not biological brothers. Mapoza was at least five years older than Themba but Themba was twice as strong and on many occasions when they fought, Themba easily overpowered Mapoza. It did not help that Mapoza was a coward at heart and he would rather run than fight.

Themba cautiously came over to Buhle and stood awkwardly a few paces away from her with his cap in hand. His face contorted as he tried to say something but all that came out was a low wailing sound. Buhle saw his fluid eyes darting around her, trying not to look directly at her. He was too humble to feast his eyes on someone as precious to him as Buhle. Themba reached in his pocket and brought out a small orange and kneeling he rolled it gently towards Buhle. Buhle smiled for the first time after the previous evening. As she got back on her feet she stopped and scooped up the orange from the ground. Smiling to Themba she said in a low and caring voice,

"It's OK Themba, I am OK. Mapoza did not hurt me". Themba dropped his shoulders in relief and started to retreat, but Buhle called out to him.

"You don't have to go, Themba. Come sit with me."

And as she said that she moved to a nearby long wooden bench and sat down at one end. She patted the space next to her, sending an invitation for Themba to sit next to her. Themba hesitated and then shyly ambled over to the bench and sat down at the opposite end of the bench. Buhle smiled at this but let him be. She was not afraid of Themba; he was the gentlest person she had known in the umuzi. He was treated as if he was an idiot by the Zulu inhabitants because he could not talk.

Themba was abandoned at birth by his unmarried mother. As soon as she was able to walk and had regained her strength after giving birth to Themba, his mother had left him in the umuzi to go live in the city. She had come to the umuzi from the city when she was almost at full term in her pregnancy. The umuzi Sangoma who also acted as the local midwife had delivered the baby and named him Bhekithemba. Themba's first cry was a squeal and the Sangoma found that Themba could not cry as a normal child since he was born with defective vocal chords. His mother was not pleased with having given birth to a child with a defect. Although he was otherwise a healthy baby she rejected him from the beginning, leaving him hungry for long periods at a time.

When the Sangoma went to check on the baby and mother a few days later, she found that the makeshift hut was empty, except for the baby. Themba was on a blanket, his clothing soaked with urine and he was just barely conscious. The Sangoma took Themba to her hut and fed and cleaned him. She had intended to find him a home with one of the other women in the umuzi but as time went on she didn't have the heart to give him away. He was such a happy contented baby and was no bother to her. She also felt that it would be good for Mapoza, her five year old son to have a brother. Mapoza however resented the intrusion of this baby into his family life and tried every trick he knew to discredit the baby in his mother's eyes. The Sangoma was a wise woman and never fell prey to her son's devious ways.

It was never known for sure whether or not Themba was also mentally retarded. Since he could not speak, Themba grew up without any education or training as did the other children in the umuzi. He was left on his own and played by himself all day long. As he grew up Themba made the umuzi inhabitants laugh with his antics and that pleased him so he continued to act silly and allow himself to be the brunt of every one's pranks. The pranks however were not physically harmful to Themba, after all the Zulus knew that he was the Sangoma's son and they dared not cross her by hurting Themba.

Themba found Buhle to be different from every one else in the umuzi. She did not make fun of him and she was kind to him. As a young man he adored and worshipped her from afar. This morning was the first time that he had been this close to her and it made the hair rise on his arms and sent shivers throughout his body. Buhle sat there and peeled the orange quietly. She could talk easily to Themba and he would listen and she knew her secret was safe with him because he would either not understand her or if he did he would not be able to repeat it. As she sat there she wondered how much she would be able to share with him. What she did not know is that her decision this morning would change the course of her life.

CHAPTER 3

Rupin was a Doctor at St Mary's Hospital in the city of Harding located on the south east coast of South Africa. It was a small hospital that provided medical care for the residents of the city of Harding. Rupin's day was not going well and now he had this to contend with. Rupin glared at the brown envelope that came in the mail to his office that day. He was hesitant to open it for deep down inside he knew the lab results would confirm what he secretly suspected. It would be another failure in a string of failures in his life that he would have to endure privately. It was as if he was paying the price for a very serious transgression in the past.

As much as he hated it, he recently seemed to always regress to reflecting on some of the major events at which he had failed. He barely made it through the final medical school exams when all his friends passed with high scores. As a doctor he was mediocre at best and felt that he had chosen the wrong profession in his life. He hated talking to sick people all day as it seemed to bring his spirits down. He knew that he was depressed and considered prescribing some anti-depressants for him self but decided against it. After all what would his peers and patients say if they found out? Rupin felt that if he corrected the root cause of his depression then things would go well.

Still holding the unopened envelope in his hand, he shuddered at what the laboratory tests results contained in the envelope would unravel. His mind imagined the look on Sheila's face, his wife, when he tells her. She was a woman with a temper and he was not sure whether he married her because he loved her or feared her. He had gone out with her a couple of times before they were married and had considered breaking off the relationship while they were dating when she had confronted him with the news. He had never seen Sheila as distraught before as she sobbed on his shoulders.

Between sobs she declared "Rupin, I am pregnant, at least eight weeks along".

Rupin was shocked, as he tried to recall when he could have been responsible for making her pregnant. He remembered a poor attempt at making love to her one evening a few months ago when she encouraged some heavy petting in the back seat of his car. Rupin in frustration had wrapped himself around her half clad body more like a wrestler than a lover and tried his best but he could not perform. It didn't help that both of them were drunk at the time. His mind was foggy and he couldn't quite remember what happened, but something must have happened because now she was pregnant. She was pregnant with his child!

As she sobbed, she said, almost reading his thoughts "there was no one else, it is you. You are the father to the child I am carrying. I want us to marry and bring this child up together."

For the first time Rupin reflected on those words. She did not say "you are the one I love" she said "I want us to marry". Did it have something to do with the fact that he was a doctor and came from a wealthy family? Rupin himself was fairly wealthy. Rupin did not think he was good looking and the huge birth mark on the side of his face did not make it any better. He had narrow shoulders and large hips with sparse facial hair. Sheila was attractive and he was honored that she had gone out with him. He was however always insecure of their relationship as she seemed to have many male friends and always had an excuse to go out with them.

At the time it was the right thing to do; he had to marry her, she was the mother of his child. The wedding was extravagant and his parents showered them with many expensive gifts. His bachelor's party was a total flop; only two of his friends attended. That fateful night after the bachelor's party, Devraj drove Rupin home. Devraj was the only friend that paid any attention to him and Rupin was somewhat possessive of him. That fateful night, Devraj decided to take a short cut through the sugar cane field. It was that fateful night that they came across the Zulu girl. The bile in Rupin's stomach rose in his chest as the memory of that evening haunted him; he did nothing wrong but he was wrong for doing nothing.

Although Rupin cherished his relationship with Devraj he hated his friend for what happened that night. They never spoke of the evening again. Devraj and he were still friends and they had continued to spend some time together. Devraj was more outgoing and had many friends and was especially popular with the girls. Rupin was envious of that and wished he could be more like Devraj. Rupin felt that he was living vicariously through Devraj's life style.

Rupin forced himself back to the present and back to that envelope. He pried open the envelope and tried to control the tremor in his hand as he slipped the paper out of the envelope. He wondered how his wife would take the news especially since her depression, having had a miscarriage. She lost the baby on her third month of her pregnancy. Rupin and she were married for barely a month now and after the miscarriage he could not get close to her. She retreated to the bedroom and stayed there for hours on end when he was home.

Rupin pulled out the single sheet of paper. The core of the lab report read:

"Based on laboratory test results of the sperm sample you provided and other tests we had conducted, we have a diagnosis for your medical condition. You have a condition known as Klinefelter Syndrome (KS). One of the symptoms of KS is minimal sperm production. This would make you infertile...."

As Rupin continued to read the words of the remaining text, his mind glazed over and he felt his legs go weak. He had to sit down as realization finally hit him. He could not have fathered that child that his wife miscarried, as he was sterile. His felt his stomach muscles contract as if he was dealt a blow to his abdomen when he realized that he had married his wife based on a lie. Tears rolled down his cheek and splattered on the lab report. The room was spinning around him and nausea overtook him. Rupin stood up and grabbed the desk for support as he made his way to the faucet at the sink in his consulting room. He filled a small paper cup with cold water and splashed his face to refresh himself. He then refilled the cup and with one swallow he downed the cold water.

Rupin went to his desk and sat down. It was late evening and he knew that he should leave to go home. But he needed to compose himself first and think through his next steps. Again he saw this as a punishment. In recent months he has had nothing but bad luck and the only positive event was his marriage to his wife. He did not want to change that since he knew that it was unlikely he would find another woman to marry him. He worked long hours and had no time or interest in the dating game. His marriage afforded a sense of convenience to his life and he wanted it to remain that way.

Rupin decided that he would not mention this lab test results to his wife. Being a doctor he knew there was something wrong with him and so he had privately taken some tests to confirm his suspicions. Throughout his early childhood and even now he was very shy, reserved and had trouble making friends. However his temper always got in the way and he would fly into rages for no apparent reason. He was unpredictable as he had many mood swings. He also lacked hair on his chest and in his teens he noticed that his breasts were slightly larger than that of his male friends. Now as an adult and being a doctor he researched the symptoms and suspected Klinefelter Syndrome as being the cause for his problems. Now he knew for sure and he knew that he could control it with testosterone hormone therapy.

He felt better that he was now able to understand himself and his emotions. Now he understood why he was so troubled about the incident in the sugar cane field. Males with the Klinefelter Syndrome had an extra X chromosome in their DNA makeup. Rupin felt that having this extra female X chromosome, he personally felt some of the violation of that night in the sugar cane field. He decided that in time he would attempt to correct the wrong that occurred, but for now he had other matters on his mind.

Oddly he felt powerful inside him for the first time after a long time. He wondered whether or not it was the knowledge of his wife's treachery that gave him the upper hand. He felt that he had handled the betrayal quite nicely. Power was like cancer for it grew inside of him. He smiled as he gathered up his files and briefcase and prepared to leave for the day. Now all he needed to do is probe a little and find out who had fathered that miscarried child. Rupin had a mission and a purpose and now for the first time he felt alive.

As Rupin locked his medical office and walked to his car he thought about his favorite US cartoonist who created Dilbert, Scott Adams, who once said, "Nothing inspires forgiveness quite like revenge".

CHAPTER 4

Eight weeks later Buhle stood at the side of the dirt road and grabbed her knees as she wrenched her stomach muscles in an effort to hurl the weak tea and bread she had for breakfast that morning. The nausea made her sick, aggravated by the fragrance of the sweet smelling rotting sugar cane that wafted over to her this morning. Normally that fragrance co-mingled with the smell of wet dew on the parched earth seemed familiar and gave her a feeling of belonging to this place. It was comforting to her for most mornings, except this one. The nausea consumed her and Buhle became very concerned. She did not want to get sick and miss work. The farmer's family especially Annie DuPlessis, has come to rely on her and she did not want to disappoint them. She steadied herself and continued on her way to work, feeling strangely alive. She could not understand this feeling as she expected to feel sick as one does when they get the flu. The only discomfort she felt was the recent tenderness in her breasts and Buhle reasoned that it was probably due to her menstrual period that was now four weeks late.

She clutched the piece of torn newspaper which was approximately four inches square and smiled. This morning when she left her home she looked expectantly at the wooden bench outside her home and was delighted to find that piece of newspaper pinned to the wooden bench. She excitedly grabbed it off the bench and looked at the pencil drawing in an area that was blank on the paper. The sketched drawing was of a dove in flight with a single rose stem in its beak. The penciled sketch was magnificent and very life like and Buhle felt special that Themba had taken the time to sketch it for her. Buhle would add this sketch to the others that Themba had done for her. Buhle had carved out a special storage place hidden in the crawl space in the DuPlessis residence utility room where she was given a bed and some personal space for her to manage.

Buhle reflected over the last eight weeks since the incident with Mapoza and with Themba coming to her rescue. She had come to know

Themba and she found that although he could not talk he had a talent in drawing. He was gifted with a pencil and he sketched animals and birds with life-like details. She also found that Themba was a sensitive and caring individual and although thought to be the umuzi idiot he was quite the opposite. In her presence she could see the depth of perception in his eyes and his drawings were done with purpose; he used them to communicate with her. It was a pity that no one had recognized his talents and assumed him to be mentally challenged just because he could not speak. Buhle remembered with a warm fondness for him the very first time she discovered a torn piece of brown paper pinned to the wooden bench just outside her home. The paper, a hand torn piece of about four inches square, torn from a brown paper bag contained a sketch of an angel tending to the foot of a lame lamb. The drawing done with a pencil was in Buhle's opinion a masterpiece and she wondered how it got there. A rustling sound from a nearby tree drew Buhle's attention to it and she found Themba, pencil still in hand, looking nervously at her for her reaction. Buhle summoned him over and thanked him for the drawing and then she lightly kissed him on the forehead. Since then Buhle received a sketch every morning and she enjoyed deciphering the meaning on her walk to work. The drawings were the high point of her day and they were always depicting some scene with domestic pets, animals and or birds. She kept every one of the drawings in her utility room crawl space storage.

Buhle and Themba had spent many hours together and their relationship flourished. Buhle enjoyed teaching Themba the basics that he so regrettably missed and he unknowingly managed to distract her from the sexual assault she had endured that evening in the sugar cane field. Themba learned to communicate with Buhle through hand gestures and drawings and Buhle discovered that he was a quick learner. The Zulus saw the relationship as a good thing as it kept Themba from bothering them. There was a cordial atmosphere in the umuzi except with Mapoza who secretly resented Themba for having snatched Buhle away from him and he was determined to not let Themba get away with it. If he could not have Buhle for himself then for sure he was not going to let Themba have her.

This morning Buhle was unusually tired when she got to work. Annie DuPlessis, the farmer's wife was outside the farm house feeding the chickens when Buhle sauntered over to her. Buhle smiled and in a cheerful voice said,

"Good morning Madam, I am sorry for being late this morning, I was not well and was sick on the way."

Annie looked at Buhle curiously. Buhle looked radiant although her cheeks were a little flushed. She did not look sick at all. Annie asked curiously,

"Did you have nausea this morning?"

Buhle looked surprised and said "Yes, Madam, how did you know?"

Annie pressed on "Do you have a boyfriend, Buhle?"

Buhle blushed and looked down. She was not accustomed to discussing personal matters with the Annie. Without looking up and shifting nervously from one foot to another, Buhle said quietly

"Yes Madam, he is a good, kind man"

Annie looked closely at Buhle and saw that her breasts were slightly enlarged and her skirt was bursting at the seams. Buhle's slim figure now showed a slight bulge in her lower abdomen area. It was obvious to Annie what the problem was. She came over to Buhle and wrapped her hands around her and hugged her and as she did she whispered gently in her ears,

"Buhle, you are pregnant. You are having a baby"

At first the words did not register. Buhle was still recovering from the unexpected show of affection and the physical contact with the Annie. As Annie drew apart, her words like a completed crossword puzzle materialized and struck her.

"Pregnant! Having a baby! Me pregnant?" The words swirled around her and she became dizzy as the full impact of the meaning hit her. Annie saw Buhle swoon and she caught her quickly and guided her to a nearby chair. Buhle sat there for a long time while Annie brought her a glass of water. Now that the realization had set in, Buhle realized that the tragedy of that terrible night was not over; in fact it had just begun.

CHAPTER 5

Themba was in good spirits this morning. In his world he had taken a big step this morning. He had drawn a dove with a single stem rose in its beak and left that for Buhle. Themba thought that Buhle would understand what message he was sending. Up to this morning the drawings were playful in nature and gave no indications of romantic advances. Today's message was clear; he had the dove and rose in the drawing as symbols for love. He was apprehensive on how she would react so he watched her from a safe hiding place and was elated to see her smile when she saw the drawing.

Themba had a lot of catching up to do. Abandoned as a child with a speech defect Themba had no birth registration documents that identified him. The Sangoma basically took him in and raised him, doing the best she could. She figured that the paper work for his identity was only necessary if he was planning to go to school or find employment. The Sangoma expected that given his handicap, Themba would be confined to the umuzi and would not seek employment and support himself. After all he was a mute and the umuzi idiot and who would employ him? She would see him aimlessly draw on scraps of paper when he was not fooling around with the other Zulu inhabitants and she was content to just see him occupied. She never looked at any one of his drawings, so she was not aware of his god given talent.

When Themba was able to walk, the Sangoma took him to the end of the umuzi perimeters and drew a line in the sand between the two trees at the entrance. With all the seriousness she could muster she warned Themba never to cross that line and leave the umuzi. She recounted several evil consequences if he ever crossed that line and left the umuzi. Over the years into adulthood, the Sangoma re-enforced the threat and consequences. Themba never had reason to disobey her. He was quite content living in the umuzi up till now. Themba was beginning to get curious about what lay outside that line especially since Buhle crossed that line everyday and came back safely. He wanted to see where she went every day.

Themba was strong and muscular with broad shoulders. Most fighters would be intimidated with Themba's physique. Themba gained his strength and muscles from being the kid at the lowest end of the totem pole. Whenever there was some renovation done in this small umuzi Themba was charged with all the hard manual labor in carrying heavy stones and buckets of mud. As his strength developed, so did the demand for more manual labor. His compensation for his hard work was the fact that he was included in the work crew and enjoyed the camaraderie of the group. Themba liked that because during those times he was treated as one of them.

Themba stood in the shade of the tree at the umuzi entrance and visions of monsters flooded his mind as he remembered the Sangoma's warning. There was no longer a line in the ground, but in Themba's mind there was not just a line in the ground but a canyon. Themba wondered how bad it could be. He was strong. He would be able to fight off almost anyone or anything. He had enough practice over the years when his friends in the umuzi ambushed him and he had to fight them off. Themba cautiously stuck one foot across the imaginary canyon and as if he was expecting to get burned, he quickly pulled it back. He waited and listened for sounds of monsters, but all he heard were the birds and insects in the background. He looked around to see if anyone was watching him and braced himself to try again. He carefully placed one foot across that imaginary canyon and although every sense in his body compelled him to pull his leg back, he firmly placed his foot on the ground across the imaginary line. He stood there for a moment expecting at any moment for the ground to open up and swallow his leg, but nothing happened. Being a little more brave, he adjusted his body such that he straddled that imaginary line and waited to be devoured. Nothing happened. Themba emitted a squeal of joy for this accomplishment as he bunny hopped along the imaginary line, one foot in the forbidden zone, and the other in his safe haven.

Themba did not want to tempt fate too much, so he carefully pulled his leg high across that line as if there was fence on the line and he had to clear it. He decided to come back the next day and try it again. He sat in the shade under the tree at the entrance and made strange sounding squeals as he expressed his version of laughter. Themba was pleased with himself as he felt that he had conquered the world. He couldn't wait to relay this to Buhle and searched his mind on how he could depict this event to her with pictures. He worshipped Buhle and she was all he could think of.

She was still on his mind an hour later when Themba got up to leave. As he stood up he noticed someone walking towards to the umuzi some distance away. Themba was surprised as it was unusual for any one to come to the umuzi during the day. Most of the folks left early in the morning and came back late in the evening. Themba thought that he must have triggered some spell and his punishment was on its way. Themba quickly ducked behind the tree and watched the figure get closer. He chastised himself for crossing that line, if only he had listened to the warnings of the Sangoma.

CHAPTER 6

Themba could not believe his eyes when he recognized the figure coming towards the umuzi. It was Buhle and she was walking with her head down and shoulders drooped. This was unusual for her as she always walked with a spring in her step, her shoulders were up and one could see the smile on her face. Themba sensed that there was a problem and wanted to run up to her, to be with her and comfort her. He dared not cross that line again because he felt that whatever had made Buhle unhappy was a result of him crossing that line. He patiently waited for Buhle to get closer to him.

Buhle was happy to see Themba under the tree and made her way to him. She took his hand and motioned him to sit beside her. Buhle's composure frightened Themba as he had never seen her like this before. Buhle looked at the ground and quietly said,

"Themba, I have a big problem, I don't know what I am going to do."

Themba looked at her, confused and now even more frightened, this did not sound good. Without waiting for a reaction Buhle continued,

"A few weeks ago one night on my way home, I was attacked by a man in the sugar cane field. Because of what happened, I am going to have a baby"

Themba's eyes widened and he creased his forehead. He did not understand what she had just said. His mind tried to digest the information and all he could piece together was that she was attacked and now she was having a baby. Tears rolled down Buhle's face and Themba's heart melted. He reached over and hugged her and then realizing what he had just done, he quickly released her. Buhle wiped her eyes and said

"I am sorry Themba, but I have to go home."

Having said that she got up and hurriedly walked home. A little distance away the Sangoma stood quietly watching the interaction between Themba and Buhle. From where she stood she could see that Buhle was pregnant and the Sangoma was angry at Themba for having made her pregnant. She summoned Themba over to her and asked,

"Is Buhle having a baby?"

Themba just heard Buhle say that she was having a baby, so he shook his head in acknowledgement. Themba did not see the Sangoma's hand come up or he would have ducked and avoided the opened handed slap across the side of his head. The Sangoma was angry with Themba; this complicated their lives. How would a dumb mute like Themba support Buhle and the baby. She hurled abuses at him,

"Themba, how could you do this to her? Now she will not be able to work and you cannot support her and the baby, you stupid boy."

Themba realized now what he had done. He was warned by the Sangoma, do not cross the line. He did not heed her warnings and now bad things are happening. The Sangoma is angry with him and most of all Buhle is sad. He was not too sure about the baby, was that good or bad? The Sangoma having expended her energy beating Themba, stormed off leaving him wondering what to do next.

He stood there for a while and pondered and then it struck him. He knew that he had to correct the wrong he created. The first thing he had to do was to go across the line at the umuzi entrance and taunt the evil spirits to find him. He figured that maybe he could offer himself to take the punishment for crossing the line and that may reverse everything. The Sangoma would be happy and Buhle will smile again. The baby, he was not sure about, he would let Buhle decide that.

Themba rushed to the imaginary line but stopped abruptly when he got to it. He cautiously placed one foot over the line and waited; nothing happened. He moved his body over the line and waited; nothing happened. Like Goofy in a cartoon movie, he brought the other leg over the imaginary fence and placed it down. He stood really still and listened. Everything was quiet, except for the sounds of insects and chirping birds. Themba felt strange, he was outside the umuzi. He looked around and saw a walking path eroded in the ground. He slowly made his way down the path, not sure in which direction he should proceed. Themba walked for quite a while until the path took him to a quiet street. Themba was intrigued at the tarred surfaces of the street and he bent over to take a closer look at the street surface. He had never seen a macadamized street surface before and did not why it was there. He stood in the middle of the street wondering what to do next when a car came hurtling towards him. Themba looked at the approaching car and was amazed at how big it looked. He had seen pictures of cars in the newspaper before but it was two dimensional and varied in size. The driver of the car blasted the horn at Themba and had to swerve to avoid hitting him. Themba just stood there not knowing what to do.

In a short while a second vehicle came down the road towards Themba. The vehicle was a small truck with a wire meshed canopy and had a long radio antenna. The door panels had the words "South African Police" stenciled on it. The small white truck stopped a short distance from Themba. Two doors opened simultaneously and two White policemen got out of the vehicle and adjusted their batons for ready deployment.

CHAPTER 7

Themba looked at the White policeman with amazement. Again he had remembered seeing pictures of policemen in the newspapers, but seeing them in the flesh surprised him. Themba had also heard of incidents in which Zulu men have been beaten by policemen and thrown into jail. Themba was not too worried, after all he thought the policemen would know that he was the son of the umuzi Sangoma and they would not dare hurt him. That vital piece of information had always worked for him in the umuzi. Little did Themba know that these policemen did not know the umuzi Sangoma and nor did they care. In fact they probably did not even know what a Sangoma was.

The two policemen, Johan and Piet, in their early twenties strode purposely towards Themba. Their hands were poised on their batons which hung by their sides hooked to their belt. Johan, the more aggressive of the two, commanded in Afrikaans,

"Var is jou pas boek, kaffir?"

Being in the late nineteen seventies in South Africa when the country was under minority white government rule, all Black South Africans had to carry a pass book which contained their identification details and a stamped approval to be out of their designated Black residential areas. Approval was given only to those who had employment outside the designated Black residential areas. Any Black South African found outside the Black residential area without the necessary approval and passbook was usually charged and taken into custody.

Themba had no paper work or identification on him and had no clue what the policemen were asking for. He did not speak Afrikaans, which was one of the official languages of South Africa at that time. The other official language was English and Themba spoke very little English, his spoken language was Zulu. The policemen saw the confusion on Themba's face and realized that he did not understand Afrikaans. Johan repeated the command in English,

"Hey Kaffir, where is your passbook?"

Themba still did not understand the command but he recognized the word "Kaffir" and he knew that it was an offensive ethnic and racial label. This derogative word was used often in addressing black South Africans. Themba knew he had to act fast, if only he could draw a picture of a Sangoma with a little boy and an arrow pointing from the Sangoma to the boy. That would explain that he was the Sangoma's son. Themba saw that one of the policemen had a pen in his shirt pocket and he figured that if the policeman lent him the pen then he could draw his picture. Themba pointed to the pen in the policeman's shirt pocket and made a squeal in an attempt to ask for the pen. Both policemen looked quizzically at each other and then burst out laughing. Here was this strong muscular black man in front of them, who looked like he could crush their skulls with his bare hands but he squealed like a pig in heat. Their laughter was really a sense of relief since when they first saw Themba they were intimated by this formidable man's presence. They relaxed their grip on their batons.

Themba became even more confused. He was used to the Zulu inhabitants laughing at him, but it was usually because of his clowning around and he usually laughed with them. Standing here in front of these policemen, he could not understand why they were laughing since he had not done anything silly to make them laugh. Themba thought that if he touched the pen in the policeman's shirt pocket then maybe the policeman would know that he wanted to borrow it, so he reached out to the policeman's shirt pocket.

Johan and Piet were already on edge and they reacted instinctively by whipping out their batons. Johan was the first to strike. He moved in and raised the baton smashing it against the side of Themba's head. Themba did not see it coming and he reeled from the impact but did not go down. The blow stunned him and he tasted his blood. Somewhat dazed but still determined to draw his picture of the Sangoma, Themba again reached for the policeman. Piet raised his baton and stepped in with a blow to Themba's upper body. Johan seeing the advancing powerful black man and incensed with fear of this man went on a rampage beating Themba repeatedly on his head and body. Amidst the squeals of pain uttered by Themba, both policemen bludgeoned him with their batons until he collapsed to the ground bleeding and unconscious.

Breathing heavily the policemen wiped the blood that had splattered onto their faces and looked at each other. Although no words were spoken between them they knew that their brutal attack on this man was unwarranted. They felt that they could justify their actions to their commanding officers; after all it was just another black man. They looked up and down the street to see if their actions were witnessed by anyone and were relieved to see the street deserted. They looked at their watches and realized that it was close to their lunch time. Again without speaking, they mutually agreed that they would surely miss their lunch break if they had to take this black man to the police station to be charged for loitering. They also knew that based on how he was lying in the side of the road he may also need medical attention. A trip to the emergency room would surely take up all their lunch time. So without looking back they got into their police vehicle and sped off leaving the dust they generated to settle on Themba's bloody body like a blanket covering the dead.

CHAPTER 8

Buhle sat on the wooden bench outside her home in the umuzi and gazed out over the fields. She was thankful to Annie DuPlessis, the farmer's wife, for giving her the day off as it afforded her the time to reflect on her situation. She did not share her experience in the sugar cane field with Annie and she had decided not to share that with anyone except Themba. As victims do, she also felt in some ways responsible for what had happened. She decided that she was going to have the baby and deal with the consequences as they come. It was late afternoon and soon the sun would set and she wondered where Themba had gone to. As she sat on the wooden bench she thought about Themba and it comforted her to know that he was part of her life. She thought about her earlier dreams of what her husband would be like and with a smile she realized that her heart had a different idea. She enjoyed teaching Themba as he was a quick learner and showed his excitement when he learnt something new. She knew that Themba was not the umuzi idiot as the Zulu inhabitants assumed. Except for his inability to speak, Themba had no other physical challenges. He was a very intelligent young man but he was very naïve and Buhle loved that about him. She found him to be sensitive and caring and completely opposite to his step-brother Mapoza.

As she sat there watching the sunset, she wished that Themba was with her to share this beautiful scene. As she wondered about Themba she had an uneasy feeling creep up her spine and she involuntarily shivered in the late afternoon heat. She went over her last conversation with Themba and a feeling of guilt slowly clouded her face and consumed her. Her last conversation with Themba was very open ended and abrupt. She was so obsessed with her feelings of the pregnancy that she had not made the effort to understand how the news would affect Themba. She chastised herself for being so heartless. How can you tell a man who cares for you that you were attacked and now you are having a baby and then just get up and walk away from him? If only she knew where Themba slept during the night she would go and look for him and make sure that he was alright. Themba moved out of the Sangoma's home when he was a teenager and spent his nights wherever his fancy took him. Since he was a grown man no one really had an interest in his whereabouts. Buhle thought that it was so sad that he was forced to be such a loner and a tear welled up in her eyes as sadness for Themba overcame her.

It was late that evening when Buhle retired to bed. She was weary and troubled since she still had not seen Themba and her worry slowly turned to panic. She tried to sleep but sleep was elusive. She tossed and turned all night and awoke at the slightest sounds. She got up early the next morning and ran outside to look for a picture on the wooden bench but there were no drawings pinned to the bench. Disappointed she got ready for work and left a message with her father for Themba, should he come around the house during the day. If anything had happened to Themba she would never forgive herself for being so cruel and selfish.

Themba sat high up on the tree branch and watched Buhle leave for work. He watched her until she was out of sight. He wanted to step down and see her but he could not do that right now. He had brought enough pain into her life by disobeying the Sangoma and crossing that line and now he had paid the price for crossing that line the second time after knowing that it was forbidden. He saw the beating he received by the police as punishment for his transgression.

He sat on the tree branch, his favorite hiding place where he could see the whole umuzi and nobody could see him. Except for Mapoza, nobody else knew of his secret hiding place. Mapoza found out about this place when he once saw Themba retreat into that spot late one evening. Mapoza did not let Themba know that he was aware of this location as he figured that this information may be useful one day. Mapoza knew that the day had come when he strolled home late last evening after drinking with friends and spotted Themba painfully climbed into his hiding spot. Mapoza decided to wait and see what develops. He was especially curious since he heard the Sangoma talk to another woman in the umuzi about Buhle being pregnant with Themba's baby. Mapoza was infuriated with the news and since then he had been plotting on how he could break up the relationship between Themba and Buhle. Mapoza wanted Buhle for himself and he felt that if he couldn't have her then no one else would.

Themba remembered recovering at the roadside after lying there unconscious for some time. When he recovered consciousness he could not stand up as he hurt all over. He knew that he must have a few fractured ribs as it hurt for him to breathe. Mustering all the strength he had, he slowly made his way to a nearby stream and washed off the blood. Every movement brought searing pain in so many parts of his body that he did not know what was injured inside of him. In the reflection of the stream he saw that his face was bruised and swollen. He was going to go into seclusion until he recovered because he did not want the Sangoma and most of all Buhle to see him like this. He had disobeyed the Sangoma and he had suffered the consequences. He made a promise to himself that he would never do that again. Even when he came back to that imaginary line hurting from the beating, he stopped and carefully stepped over it so as to not disturb it. The potency of that line was firmly implanted in his head. That was in the past; for now he had to rest and recover in his safe haven suspended way above the ground.

That evening Buhle passed below that tree on her way home after work. Little did she know that Themba was lovingly watching her from his safe hiding place up in the tree branches. She had her head bent over and her eyes focused on the ground, sadness had totally engulfed her. She had a bad feeling in the pit of her stomach that Themba was hurting and she had no way to go help him.

Mapoza knew that Themba would have to come down from the tree periodically, so he hid himself in a nearby hut and waited. During the daytime Themba knew that Buhle had gone to work and almost all the others were either at school or at work. At this time he checked to make sure no one was around before he descended from the tree and made his way to the nearby stream. Mapoza followed him at a safe distance and watched him clean himself at the river and then get some half ripened mangos from the tree for nourishment. From where he stood he saw the bruises on Themba's face and noticed how painfully and deliberately Themba moved. Mapoza wondered how Themba got hurt and mused that whoever attacked him would have to be a giant to do that to Themba and live to walk away. When Mapoza was certain that Themba was getting ready to return to his tree he casually strolled towards Themba and acted surprised to see him. Themba was shocked to see Mapoza as he expected him to be at the city this time of day. Themba tried to hide his face but it was too late, Mapoza was already a few feet away. Themba squealed with embarrassment and he sounded like a pig being slaughtered. Mapoza grinned at this as he had never seen Themba's spirit beaten down this way since he was always squealing with laughter. Mapoza feigned concern as he pointed to Themba's face for explanation.

It took quite a few tries for Mapoza to understand somewhat, what had happened. Crossing the imaginary line was simple to communicate as Mapoza was present when the Sangoma drew the line in the ground. Although Mapoza understood the reasons for Themba not to cross the line, he conveniently did not explain it to Themba when he became an adult. Mapoza always suspected that Themba was intelligent and an excellent artist but he did not want to broadcast that and draw attention to his step brother. Mapoza walked away with the understanding that two uniformed White men beat him for crossing the line. Mapoza smiled when he saw the reaction he got when he mentioned Buhle. It was obvious that Themba did not want Buhle to see him like this. Mapoza was not able to get anything from Themba about the baby and Mapoza concluded that Themba was not comfortable talking about Buhle and the baby. Mapoza envied and resented Themba on being the father to Buhle's baby but he did not show it. Mapoza left Themba and walked away so that Themba could return to his hiding place. He did not want to compromise that hiding place as he wanted Themba to be out of the way while he did his mischief.

CHAPTER 9

A small Zulu umuzi lives and breathes like a massive organism. Its tranquility is a reflection of the inhabitant's state of mind and their peaceful existence in their everyday routine of life. The umuzi Sangoma goes about her usual routine ensuring that the spirits are appeased and generally keeps the peace. When Mapoza decided to interfere with Buhle and Themba's relationship, he unwittingly set into motion a chain of events that would have devastating consequences.

The next morning Mapoza waited for Buhle to leave for work. As she emerged from her hut he saw her go to the wooden bench and scan it carefully looking for something. Mapoza had no idea what she was looking for and he did not care, he had a plan to put into motion. Buhle saw Mapoza saunter over to her and she cringed at having to engage into a conversion with him. Mapoza put on his best charming smile, exposing a set of yellow tobacco stained teeth.

"May I walk a little way with you?" he chirped. He continued without waiting for an answer, "I want to tell you about Themba."

The mention of Themba's name snapped Buhle into attention. "Is he OK, where is he?" she inquired urgently.

"Themba is OK" Mapoza retorted, a little annoyed at her concern for Themba.

Mapoza looked intently at Buhle and could not help admiring her. She looked radiant in the early morning sun, her pregnancy bringing some color to her cheeks and the whites of her eyes glistened like dew drops in the morning sun. Mapoza wanted to take her into his arms and hold her, but he had to play this out carefully.

Still engaging her eyes, Mapoza said softly

"Themba is angry with you for having the baby".

Mapoza saw the sudden flash of hurt in her eyes and he continued quickly, going in for the kill.

"Themba says that you were selfish, knowing his handicap, you put him in a difficult situation. He does not want to see you again and wants you to stay away from him."

Buhle's heart sank and her knees buckled. She felt like her heart was torn from her chest; she wanted to die. Mapoza seeing her weaken, quickly grabbed her before she sank to the ground and hugged her awkwardly. Buhle did not resist, she was beaten, she did not care; Themba was not coming back to her. Tears rolled down her cheek as she sobbed quietly. Mapoza let her go but placed one arm across her shoulders and gently walked her down the path. Mapoza taking advantage of Buhle's weakened state said,

"Don't worry, I will take care of you, I will not let you suffer because of my stepbrother's cowardly nature."

Buhle had withdrawn inwardly shutting off the world around her and she did not even register what Mapoza had just said. She was numb with grief and Mapoza like a predator, going in for the kill, had sensed her weakened state. He wanted so desperately to take her down and have her for himself but he dared not do that for he knew that although Themba could not hear him he was watching him from his hiding place in the tree.

Themba watched intently from his secret hiding spot high up in the tree and tried to figure out what was transpiring on the ground. As hard as he tried, he could not hear what was said although he could see both of them together. Themba figured that Mapoza had shared with Buhle that he was hurt but OK and based on her reaction Mapoza was consoling her. Themba was so proud of his step brother; he was helping Buhle to be strong while Themba recovered from his injuries.

As Mapoza walked the numbed, grief stricken Buhle out of sight, he wanted to take advantage of her but resisted the temptation. He savored the time when she would submit to him willingly and then she would be his conquest. Mapoza walked with her part of the way to the farm house and watched her go to work. She looked so sad and beaten that he almost felt sorry for her. But he had no time for such sentiments as he was too busy plotting his next step. When Buhle disappeared from sight Mapoza doubled back to the umuzi to meet with Themba. He knew that Themba would be waiting for news from him and he definitely had news to share.

Themba was anxious for Mapoza to return to hear what Buhle had said. He was so impatient that on more than one occasion he almost fell off the tree trying to peer around the branch looking for his stepbrother. When he saw Mapoza skip down the dusty pathway his heart lurched in anticipation and he scurried down the tree trunk to greet his step-brother.

When Mapoza saw Themba hurry across to him he feigned a worried look on his face. Themba saw Mapoza's face and he halted in his tracks, he sensed that the news was bad. Themba's pig-like squeal was pitiful and even Mapoza had a fleeting moment of pity for him. Mapoza grabbed Themba by the shoulders and faced him. He looked deeply into Themba's inquiring eyes and said in a low voice,

"She does not want to see you again."

Themba's eyes expressed surprise and foreboding that he felt deep inside of him. Themba gripped Mapoza's hand tightly as if he could squeeze the explanation out of him. Mapoza squirmed under the pressure but mustered up the courage to continue.

"She says it is all your fault and wishes she never met you"

Themba felt the words pierce his heart and he wailed in disbelief. Mapoza sensing an opening to bring this big brute down said with a stern voice.

"She wants you to stay away from her, never see her again; she wants you to go away. She says that it was your fault this happened to her"

Themba staggered away and all Mapoza could hear was a hissing squealing sound that Themba made when he cried as a baby. Mapoza stood there watching Themba's trembling form bent over and he was amazed how easily he was able to reduce this formidable man to a weak pitiful child.

Themba had never felt so alone in all his life. He was so much happier when he fooled around as the umuzi idiot. Now that he has allowed himself to grow and love another, he became a victim of his desires. Anger rose in his chest, he hated himself for what he had done to Buhle. If only he had listened to the Sangoma and not crossed that line none of this would have happened. He clutched at his clothes as if ripping it off would remove the curse of the "line in the ground". Not being able to take it anymore, the mental anguish tearing into his soul, Themba took off like a startled rabbit and tore down the field towards that river. He knew from the Sangoma that the angry spirits lurked along the river's edge and he wanted to sacrifice himself so that peace would return to the umuzi. That river always provided him comfort, especially watching it cascade over the rocky waterfall. He could be like that free falling droplets of water suspended in space, without a care in the world. Themba wanted to be free of pain and guilt.

CHAPTER 10

Rupin stood at his lounge window and watched Devraj leave his home and get into his car that was parked in the driveway. They never spoke of that night in the sugar cane field and Rupin wondered whether Devraj had any regrets about it. The incident had created a wedge between them but yet it bonded them together. It seemed like Devraj stayed around Rupin as he needed him to condone his action in the sugar cane field and ease his conscience. Rupin and Devraj had little in common and their visits with each other became obligatory. Rupin noticed that Devraj was more comfortable talking with his wife, Sheila and this evening he thought that he saw Devraj smile secretly at Sheila.

Now as he watched Devraj drive away he started to wonder whether there was anything going on between Sheila and his friend. Having planted that suspicion in his fertile mind, it started to grow like a weed. He wondered whether Devraj and Sheila were lovers before he married her. Like a meteorite crashing into earth, it struck him; what if it was Devraj who had made her pregnant? Rupin suddenly went weak and he had to sit down on his couch as he recounted the events of the past.

Rupin knew that Sheila and Devraj were friends and he also was aware that at the time she told him that she was pregnant; Sheila and Devraj were not on speaking terms. Rupin now also knew that Sheila would look for financial security and since Rupin was a Doctor and came from a wealthy family, she would prefer to snag him into marriage. Devraj on the other hand was from a poor family. He did not further his studies and jumped from one menial job to another. He had no ambitions to make something of himself and did not offer a girl much security in marriage

Rupin was startled back to reality when the shrill sound of the telephone pierced the air. The distraction served him well since this mental probing had caused the muscles in his face to twitch and he was beginning to hyperventilate. Rupin grabbed the phone as if it was the source of his anxiety and angrily said,

"Yes, what is it?"

The voice at the other end was a nurse at the emergency room of St Mary's Hospital. She spoke in hurried tones,

"We have an emergency at the hospital. A Zulu man was just brought in by taxi. He is experiencing chest pains and is having difficulty breathing. His daughter who brought him in said that he has been unwell for a few days." She continued without prompting,

"Doctor, he does not look good, would you please hurry?"

Rupin was on the staff at St Mary's Hospital that served the local community as well as the local Zulu population from the nearby villages in cases of emergency. It was not common for the Zulu villagers to use the hospital as the Sangoma usually took care of most of the medical problems with customary herbs and spiritual blessings. Periodically there would be a case when a Zulu patient would be brought in, when the efforts of the Sangoma proved to be in vain. This was one of those cases and Rupin knew that it was serious. He gathered his satchel and car keys and prepared to leave.

Rupin called out to Sheila to let her know that he was leaving but she did not respond. Rupin knew that she had heard him and he was accustomed to the indifference in her. A new emotion grabbed his stomach and twisted it into a knot. Would she call Devraj as soon as he left for the hospital? Rupin hated how he felt as he was poisoning himself with his suspicions. As Rupin passed the hallway mirror he took a minute to straighten his collar and run his fingers through his hair. As he did that he noticed how dark the birthmark on the side of his face looked. That birthmark acted like a stress meter; Rupin knew that it darkened whenever he was stressed and it was especially true at this time.

******

The ancestral spirits of the Zulu village were restless. The Sangoma was especially worried as she cast her eyes at the dark clouds swirling in the afternoon skies. She wore her ceremonial garment this afternoon as it afforded her a sense of power over the nervous villagers. She also felt that it appeased the spirits and at this time she needed all the favors she could get from the ancestral spirits.

The Sangoma was summoned to Buhle's hut. When she received the call, she had a foreboding feeling that this was only the beginning of their problems. The ancestral spirits were definitely restless; she felt it in her bones. She had not seen Themba for at least a month and thought about her last encounter with him. She had struck him across the face and chastised him for making Buhle pregnant. She figured that he was probably sulking and sooner or later he would return. She was still angry with him for his irresponsibility but blamed Buhle for allowing it to happen. Buhle also had changed recently; she was no longer the happy jovial young lady. Buhle was withdrawn and walked with her eyes downcast and never smiled. Mapoza was also acting strangely. He seemed to be hanging around Buhle more these days and seemed to be up to no good.

The Sangoma had been called to Buhle's hut several times recently to tend to Buhle's father who complained about chest pains. The Sangoma's chants and herbal concoctions did little to relieve him of these pains. Now the Sangoma was convinced that the spirits want to take him away as a token for Buhle's stupidity for having Themba's baby. Buhle was desperate; she did not want to lose her father. Her father was all she had and she suspected that the stress of her having a baby had induced the discomfort in his chest. As a last resort she managed to talk one of the villagers to help take him to the nearby hospital emergency room at St Mary's. The journey by a local taxi service was traumatic to her father and she sucked in a breath every time he clutched at his chest in agony. The taxi was a white beaten up Toyota HiAce ten seat passenger carrier, filled to capacity with sixteen passengers. She could see her father struggle to breathe in the cramped hot and humid interior of the vehicle.

They finally got to the emergency room and the attendants put her father on a stretcher and wheeled him in for treatment. Buhle was not allowed to be with him. She sat in the waiting room wringing her hands in worry. From her seat in the waiting room she saw activity in the emergency room and the urgency at which the attending doctors rushed around and the barked out orders from the Doctors only heightened her nervousness. As she gazed at the reception desk she caught sight of a familiar face. It was the birth mark on his face that drew her attention to him. She recognized and remembered it from the passenger in the car that awful night in the sugar cane field. Buhle quickly turned away so that he would not see her.

Now it dawned on her who the passenger was since she had seen him at the hospital before and knew him from that birth mark. Afraid that he might see her Buhle retreated to the far corner of the room and grabbed a magazine to cover her face. She stayed out of site until he left the reception area.

Exhausted from the day's events, Buhle fell off to sleep in her chair and lost all the worries of the day. Several hours later Buhle's peaceful sleep was disturbed by a nurse who asked Buhle to accompany her. Buhle still groggy from her sleep did her best to stay with the fast walking nurse, as she zigzagged between the busy corridors of this emergency room. Finally they got to an empty room and the nurse turned to Buhle and with a cool composure of a professional she said.

"Buhle your father had a massive heart attack and there was nothing we could do for him. He expired about twenty minutes ago, I am sorry for your loss"

Buhle was speechless as she repeated each word in her mind until she understood its meaning. Even then she thought that she had heard wrong. She looked up at the nurse to ask her to repeat what she had just said but the nurse was already on her way back to the reception area leaving Buhle alone with her misery.

CHAPTER 11

The Sangoma took the passing away of Buhle's father as an omen that the spirits were angry and needed to be appeased. The Sangoma had concluded that Themba had obviously deserted the village when faced with responsibilities of a baby. She instructed Buhle to marry Mapoza who was willing to take care of her and the baby. Buhle was so distraught and alone that she did not care anymore and humbly succumbed to the Sangoma's request. Mapoza celebrated this event by spending the night with his friends at the brew hall getting drunk. Mapoza was ecstatic for another reason; he did not have to provide lobolla for Buhle as she was now an orphan. Lobolla was the price a man had to pay to the father for marrying his daughter and the price was usually in livestock. In the case where the prospective bride had borne a child thus proving that she is fertile, the price of lobolla was increased. Mapoza now did not have to worry about that since Buhle's father was dead.

Mapoza was however not satisfied. His prized trophy, Buhle, had somehow tarnished in his eyes and with her pregnancy she had lost that luster. He felt cheated, the trophy was handed to him and that did not do anything for his ego. He did not earn it. He could not boast to his friends on how he had seduced the most desired girl in the village. In addition she was carrying Themba's baby and he found it difficult to be aroused sexually by her in her pregnant condition. He had visualized flirting with her and enjoying many drug induced hours of drunken sex. Now her eyes were blank and she showed no emotion, the fire in her life had fizzled out. The only time she showed some emotion is when she lovingly touched her ever expanding stomach. She loved that unborn baby more than she loved him, and that really infuriated him since that baby was a remnant of Themba. That was one of the reasons he did not touch Buhle; she was tainted.

Mapoza wanted to walk away from this commitment, but then he would have to answer to his mother the Sangoma and that, he was not prepared to do. Mapoza sat under this mango tree and watched the line of ants cross his path as they went about their daily tasks. Using the point of a small twig he selected every fifth ant and crushed it. This mindless task provided the focus he needed to think through his dilemma. As he destroyed ant after ant creating mayhem amongst the remaining ants he wished he could wipe out the life of the one thing that stood between him and Buhle; Themba's baby. The thought hit him so hard that he slapped his forehead with astonishment, forgetting that he had the twig in his hand. The twig missed his eye but gorged a piece of his flesh from his head. Enduring the searing pain that accompanied the tearing skin, he smiled triumphantly. He would make sure that Buhle aborts the baby, whether she agrees to it or not. After all he was the man and she has to do his bidding.

Mapoza summoned up the courage to talk to Buhle that evening, but just in case he needed it, he went to the beer hall to drink a few ijubas, his favorite sorghum beer, to help out. That night after Buhle came home from work and had gone to bed, Mapoza staggered towards her hut and when he arrived there he stood outside and sucked in the cool air to clear his mind. The doorway entry to the hut was typically short so that one had to kneel to enter the hut. This was designed to put an attacker at a disadvantage when he entered a hut. Mapoza had no intentions of kneeling to enter the hut as he was sure that in his drunken state he would fall over. He instead picked up his right leg to kick the door open and as he did that he staggered and had to take two steps backwards to regain his balance. On his second try his boot connected and the door flung open.

Buhle jumped out of her bed terrified and crawled up to the back wall. She heard Mapoza's drunken voice calling her and she immediately clutched at her night clothing protectively. She asked herself "what did he want now?" She was confused as he had not touched her or come to her hut after her father had died and that was indeed a blessing. Regaining her composure she draped a shawl across her shoulders and went outside the hut to see what Mapoza wanted.

Mapoza was having difficulty standing in one spot and as a result could not easily focus on Buhle's face. He hiccupped once and with his eyes swimming in its sockets he pointed to the bulge in her abdomen and slurred'

"You need to get rid of that thing or else I will do it for you."

Mapoza tried to glare at Buhle as he made that demand but he couldn't stand long enough in one spot. He also wondered when she grew so tall and menacing. Her eyes that were recently blank seemed to be ablaze. He was expecting to see her head explode at any minute now and unconsciously took a step back. Her eyes pierced his with so much of venom that he had to look away. The sound of a door slamming was all he heard when he looked back. She had gone back into her hut without uttering a word, but yet she spoke volumes.

Now that she had gone, Mapoza felt safe again but he was not done with this baby. His drunken mind explored different options on how best to kill that growing fetus and reclaim his prize.

It was almost midmorning when Mapoza opened his eyes the next day. He did not want to think about his encounter with Buhle the night before; it scared him. He figured that a mother was awarded superhuman strength by spirits when she had to defend a young one. Now that he was away from her he figured that he could take her down if he wanted to, after all he was a man. That line of thought gave him an idea; he could wear a disguise and attack her on her way home from work. A quick kick or two at her belly would do the trick. That will teach her to disobey him and that baby would be out of his life for good.

That evening Buhle casually made her way home from work. The path through the sugar cane field looked more ominous in the dark than she could remember and she was a little apprehensive. She looked over her shoulders a couple of times but saw nothing although she had the uncanny feeling that she was being stalked. Ever since her father had died she resorted to keeping a journal to keep her sanity. She recounted the events that led to her having the baby and most of all she wrote about Themba. The journal had many conversations with Themba as if he was still with her. She found this to be very therapeutic and allowed her to keep her spirits up for the sake of the baby. She was thankful for her private hiding place in the farmer's utility room as it allowed her to hide the journal there. She did not want Mapoza to ever find that journal. She was reflecting on the previous night when Mapoza came to her hut when she heard a rustling in the sugar cane field.

Buhle stopped in her track, her senses heightened. She listened carefully and the rustling stopped. Buhle broke out in a sweat; she was suspicious since if the rustling was made by an animal then it would not have stopped when she stopped walking. She considered running but was afraid that she would fall and hurt the baby.

Buhle tip toed forward but realized that was ridiculous. She walked with renewed urgency hoping that all this was just her imagination. As she rounded a corner she heard more rustling and this time it was close; she knew that it was not her imagination. She stopped and peered into the darkness of the sugar cane field but saw nothing. As she straightened up, a dark figure lunged out of the darkness and knocked her to the ground. As she fell she grabbed her stomach protectively twisting as she fell, landing on her side and then rolled on to her back. The dark figure swung around and came back at her with his feet raised. Buhle cried out, pleading for her baby. Buhle turned her back to the attacker and assumed a fetal position and prepared for the worst. Her fetal position underscored that of her baby's, protecting it from that vicious blow. The attacker frustrated that he did not have a clear shot at her abdomen, jumped over her and prepared to follow through with his diabolical plan to destroy that baby.

CHAPTER 12

André Pretorius looked at the empty bed, still perfectly made and not slept in, and his heart sank. He knew that this day would come and even after being with him for a few weeks, his departure was difficult to accept. André knew that he was free to go when ever he was ready. André was happy that Themba had progressed so well and was ready to leave but he selfishly wished that he would have stayed a little longer.

André sat down on the edge of the bed and pulled one of the many sketches pinned to the wall and ran his finger across the drawing. His mind drifted to the past few weeks and a tear wet his eye and rolled down his cheek.

André remembered that morning so clearly. He was at the KwaZulu Natal School for the Deaf when he received the tragic news of his wife's untimely death. The next few weeks after he buried his wife was a haze and he recalled taking his companion and four legged best friend, his German Sheppard named Misty and headed to his cabin in the hills.

André remembered clearly that day as if it happened just yesterday. He was strolling down the river's edge to clear his mind with his trusted friend, Misty when at a distance he saw a young Zulu man standing at the edge of the waterfall. The man stood precariously at the edge of the waterfalls agitated about something. Andre feared that he was going to fall over the edge.

André froze, rooted to the spot, as he saw the Zulu man, who he now knew was Themba, stumble and almost fall in. Misty, without any warning darted forward and with a few strides reached the young man and grabbed a piece of his shirt pulling him off the rocks. Both of them fell into the fast flowing water. Themba with his strong powerful arms grabbed a rock with one hand and with the other he wrapped his arm around the dog. With strong powerful strokes Themba swam against the strong current and beached themselves on the river's edge.

Themba turned and faced the dog and André was afraid of what he would do next. To his surprise Themba reached over and patted the dog. The interaction between man and dog was cordial and André relaxed. André stood and watched the two of them for a while longer. He did not want to scare Themba away. Themba got out of the water and headed to the banks of the river with Misty following him, wagging his tail in delight. When they got to the bank the dog rocked his body to shed off the excess water spraying it all over Themba. He heard Themba squeal like a pig in laughter and André recognized the sounds coming from him.

André had spent a lifetime teaching dumb and mute children and adults the art of sign language. The sounds made by Themba were those that would be uttered by a dumb person with a defective larynx. Through the years he had become very familiar with that sound as he taught these unfortunate souls the art of signing.

Themba sat on the banks of the rivers edge stroking the dog affectionately. They had become instant friends and André's heart warmed to see such a union. Without attracting attention André approached Themba and sat down next to him. Themba recoiled, expecting to be struck by this stranger, who to Themba was a White man and who in his opinion was a threat. Themba was about to get up and retreat from this stranger when André held up his right hand in a greeting gesture and then using the same hand he formed a "hello" with his lips and morphed the word into sign language.

Themba looked at André quizzically and his initial reaction of fear transformed to one of confusion. Themba felt that the ancestral spirits had sent this man and his dog in answer to his pleas. Offering him a piece of Biltong as comfort food, André beckoned him to follow him. Biltong was a piece of dried meat seasoned and salted and resembled beef jerky. To Themba the biltong was a delicacy and since he was starving he relished the meat.

Themba and André walked side by side with Misty following them closely. André was careful not to make any audible sounds but continued to use sign language to communicate. Themba found this silence to be very comforting and he was starting to relax with this stranger. His first experience with a white man was traumatic and the beating he received from the white policeman had scarred his memory. This white man however was kind and gentle and he felt he could trust him.

André lead Themba to his cabin in the foothills, a modest building he had maintained for his weekend fishing getaways. The cabin was a comfortable structure with two beds and a primitive kitchen and toilet facilities. When they got there Themba inspected the cabin curiously and smiled broadly with approval. Andre boiled some water and prepared a lamb stew while Themba watched attentively. Andre never stopped smiling and worked silently but engaged Themba's eyes frequently letting Themba know that he was a friend. They enjoyed a quiet meal together while the dog chewed on a lamb bone at their side.

After dinner André gestured to the bed and encouraged Themba to sleep in it. To show that he trusted him André climbed into the other bed and in sign language wished Themba goodnight. Themba was not sure what to do as he was not accustomed to having company at bed time. The events of the day and the trauma he had gone through had made him weary and the fatigue overcame him. As the darkness closed around him, Themba succumbed to his fatigue and gave in to peaceful sleep. The next morning Themba got up startled for he was in unfamiliar surroundings but the warm body of the sleeping German Sheppard dog besides him calmed him down. The smell of fried bacon filled the cabin and made him salivate. He felt comfortable and for the first time he felt safe. André greeted him silently with sign language and his warm eyes conveyed to Themba that he was a friend.

That was the beginning of a precious friendship that lasted several weeks. Andre spent those weeks teaching Themba the art of sign language and found him to be a fast learner. Themba for his part drew many sketches and shared his life's story through the combination of drawings and sign language. They got to know each other and learned that each of them had emotional burdens to deal with. They discovered that each of them was running away from their problems. André saw Themba grow and mature emotionally and mentally. Each day he became more confident and walked taller. Themba also learned that he had been under the wrong perceptions regarding the "line crossing" and Buhle's pregnancy. With controlled anger he realized that Mapoza had taken advantage of his ignorance and it was at that time that he silently decided to remedy the situation.

André also knew that Themba's time with him was coming to an end. They had become very close friends and he hated to see him leave.

He wondered whether he would see Themba again. Although he knew that Themba would leave, seeing his empty bed this morning saddened him. As he sat on the edge of the bed, reflecting over the past months Misty came over to him. Misty also experiencing the loss, licked André's hand before laying its long nose on his master's thigh and whimpered.

CHAPTER 13

History was repeating itself. A few months ago at this same sugar cane field there were cries for help and pleadings to stop. The cries were in vain for a life was conceived. Now the same cries and pleadings fragmented the air, but this time the cries were to save that conceived life.

Mapoza, disguised to conceal his identity, was becoming frustrated. He could not get an opening for good kick to her abdomen since in her fetal position she protected the baby. Mapoza bent over and grabbed her by the shoulders and roughly turned her over. In doing so he positioned himself over her to stomp on her stomach. He was determined to end this interference in his life.

Buhle was crying and begging, pleading for the baby's life. She did not care about her own life, she pleaded for the attacker not to harm the baby. Buhle was desperate but with every passing second she knew that the end was near. Suddenly a dark figure shot past her like a freight train, and tackled Mapoza driving him down away from her. At first Buhle thought that it was an animal for it moved so quietly but with purpose. Buhle's fear morphed into one of confusion as she watched this second person grab Mapoza and lift him over his head and then bodily throw him into the sugar cane field. She heard Mapoza cry out in pain as he hit the dirt followed with a sound of a bone breaking. Mapoza's cry in pain changed to begging for mercy but the dark figure pounded Mapoza like a punching bag. Buhle was wide eyed with surprise and then anger filled her when she recognized Mapoza as her attacker. She gasped as Mapoza got up and scurried away on one leg dragging along his other broken leg.

Buhle strained her eyes at the dark figure that had saved her. The man built strongly was now heading towards her. She stiffened in apprehension and now sitting on her buttocks, she brought her legs close to body and hugged them forming a defensive ball, burying her head into her locked arms. As the dark figure closed in on her, she drew in a breath as the figure bent down and gently caressed her shoulder. She risked one glance at this figure and to her utter surprise she recognized the face. It was Themba's smiling face. The rest of him did not resemble Themba for this man walked with a confident stride with shoulders upright and head proudly held up.

Buhle dared not breathe for fear of losing this vision that she was hoping was not a figment of her imagination. Themba reached down and lovingly picked her up in his arms. She looked into his eyes and saw the deep love and caring that Themba had for her. She knew it was her Themba and not a mirage. She buried her head in his muscular chest and her tears flowed in a mixture of relief and gratitude for his return. With ease Themba carried her part of the way as she composed herself. When he set her down they walked hand in hand in silence. Buhle did not need to ask questions, she knew he was back and she felt the power of his presence.

When they got to her hut, Buhle invited Themba to stay with her and it was the first time that she noticed that Themba was communicating with hand signals. Buhle was curious as to how he had learned that technique. She did not know hand signals but she knew that she would learn the technique very soon.

That night Themba sat by her bedside and watched her sleep. They did not want to spend time trying to understand what had happened over the last few weeks. There was plenty of time for that.

The next morning Buhle and Themba were startled by a commotion in the village. Both of them went outside to see what all the shouting was about. Like a tornado the Sangoma was on a war path leaving the early risers in the village running for safety, out of her path, as she marched towards Buhle's hut. It was obvious that Mapoza had made it home and recounted to his mother, the Sangoma his version of what had happened.

Themba and Buhle sat on the wooden bench outside the hut and watched with amused interest the tornado like approach of the Sangoma. Mapoza watched at a safe distance. Still enraged, the Sangoma approached Themba and Buhle but her rage drained slowly into curiosity and surprise. She recognized Themba but he looked strangely calm and composed. Themba rose to his feet and the Sangoma stopped in her tracks as his shadow engulfed her. Themba seemed to tower over her. The Sangoma's anger drained and was replaced by fear of this formidable person in front of her. The villagers who earlier scurried into hiding places poked their heads out to catch a glimpse of how this conflict would play out.

The Sangoma recognized that she would lose her credibility amongst the villages if she lost the confrontation with Themba. She raised her arms to the skies as if the spirits of the forefathers had summoned her. She mumbled some unintelligible phrases and started swaying to the beat some frenzied melody playing in her head. During her chanting she very cleverly relayed to all that gathered around her that the spirits were angry and much groveling would be needed for peace to return to the village. She went on to say that she was asked to arrange the necessary sacrifices and gifting. Having sufficiently perturbed the crowds she turned on her heels and stormed off. The local Zulu inhabitants of this village dispersed leaving Themba and Buhle alone with their thoughts.

There was so much to talk about and so much to explain, but their presence to each other seemed to be sufficient for now. Themba seemed to make himself understood easily, especially with the combination of hand signing, his facial expressions and sketches. Buhle wept with joy and relief. For the first time after a long time she was happy. Her excitement spurred the baby into activity and Buhle took Themba's hand and placed it on her abdomen to feel the baby's movement. The smile on Themba's face did not need words to describe the joy he felt although he knew that the baby was not his. He made a promise to himself that he was going to take care of the baby and Buhle.

Mapoza watched his mother the Sangoma return with a defeated look on her face. He went up to her to find what she planned to do, but she shoved him out of the way and retreated into her hut, still mumbling curses under her breath. Mapoza, afraid to go near Themba thought about the transformation. It was as if the spirits of his forefathers had given Themba, Herculean powers. Mapoza considered his predicament; he had lost his chances with Buhle and he was in pain. He also considered the possibility that Themba may come looking for him because of his attempts to kill the baby. Mapoza was not about to give in. He knew that he could not physically take Themba down so he decided to do what he did best. Mapoza would get other people to do his bidding by cleverly manipulating them into action.

The Sangoma sat in her smoke filled hut and in a trance threw small bones repeatedly onto a small mat. She was summoning the spirits for guidance on this abuse on her reputation. As she rocked back and forward, chanting in unison her eyes bulged with frenzy. A diabolical plan was hatching in her head. It was desperate and traumatic and would shake the very core of each of the villagers but she knew that it was time to regain control. This required some careful preparation if she was to be successful. It was critical that although the deed was drastic she needed the villagers to support her as this matter could go all the way up to the King of the Zulu's. The Sangoma now in a trance, her eyes still rolled up to the back of her head, slowly got up and steadied herself. She slowly and deliberately went to the entrance of the hut. She stood at the entrance, drooling saliva over her beads on her chest, and raised her hands in thankful prayer to the angry spirits. They would be pleased with her gift to them.

Mapoza saw the figure of the Sangoma darken the entrance of the hut and a cold bony hand gripped his heart and squeezed. He sank to the ground in sheer fear of the apparition in front of him and for the first time he was terrified by the transformation he saw in his mother.

CHAPTER 14

Rupin noticed that Sheila his wife was starting to get restless. They had been married now for several months and she was bored, she wanted to start a family. He came to that conclusion by watching how she reacted to little children that she came across. Her eyes would light up and she would get on her knees and play with them. Rupin also knew that he could not father a child with Sheila for two reasons. The most obvious was the fact that they did not share any intimate moments and he could not remember when last they were intimate. She always pretended to be asleep when he came to bed and she did the same when he got up in the morning. That did not bother him as he did not have the desire anyway, a consequence of his medical condition. This fact he kept private to himself.

Over the last few months Devraj did some serious soul searching and in looking in the mirror he hated what he saw. Devraj was in his early twenties with a boyish charm. Living in this small town he quickly realized that his boyish good looks and easy going nature were all he needed to attract girls. What attracted the girls the most were his eyes. His eyes were deep and mysterious with a hint of mischief and the girls would love to stare into them. The eyes combined with his boyish charm served him very well.

Devraj was not very bright but he did well for himself from day to day and lived for the moment. He worked when he needed money and did not hold on to a job for any length of time. Over the last few months, Devraj found it comfortable to spend time with Rupin and Sheila. Devraj knew that Rupin was a loner and at first he spent time with him because he had nothing better to do. The incident at the sugar cane field was an impulsive move on Devraj's part. He had taken some drugs that evening for the first time and was drunk at the time and was really feeling reckless. At the time he had not thought about the consequences of his actions; he was being a dare devil. The next morning when he sobered up the events of the previous evening came flooding back and he wondered whether it was a nightmare or did it really happen. Devraj got up that morning and arranged to meet with Rupin. Devraj planned to see if he could deduce what really happened without coming outright and asking Rupin.

His time spent with Rupin was a little awkward and Devraj felt that Rupin was over compensating. Devraj was convinced that the incident actually happened. That was when the guilt set in and the torment began. Devraj would sit, alone with his thoughts, trying to decide what he should do. He could look for the girl and if he found her, what would he say; "I am sorry for what I did to you"?

Devraj realized that if he went to the Zulu village to look for the girl, he would be killed by the locals if they found out what he did. Going to the police would also be futile as they would not care especially if the girl did not report the crime. Devraj considered all the options in front of him and settled on the one in which he would pretend it never happened. That was the easiest option to go with but it was the hardest for him to deal with. His guilt and conscience tormented him and sleep was difficult. Whether or not he liked it, he was welded to Rupin by this secret.

So Devraj continued to visit Rupin on a regular basis and they continued a strange friendship. This relationship would have been impossible had it not been for Sheila. She was like a buffer between him and Rupin. Devraj renewed his friendship with Sheila especially since she had distanced herself away from him during the last year. Devraj never did understand what he had done to make her so mad that she would walk away from him without explanation. Devraj was even more confused especially since he thought that they were having a good time together including some very intimate times when he made love to her. At that time Devraj felt that he had found the girl he would like to marry and settle down with. When she ditched him and married Rupin, Devraj was angry but tolerated Rupin enough to be close to him so that he would be close to Sheila. It was only when Sheila left him did Devraj realize that he had feelings for her. Sheila never told Devraj that she was pregnant with his baby.

And so this odd couple co-existed, each one of them having a secret that bonded them together. Often Devraj would visit Rupin and Sheila in the evenings and they would hang out together. Although Rupin was a physician at the hospital he also had to do emergency duty at the hospital's emergency room for one week every month. So during these weeks when he got an emergency call he would return to the emergency room and would have to leave Sheila and Devraj alone at his house. These times took its toll on Rupin as he anguished over what was happening whilst he was gone. Rupin realized that he was his own worst enemy. What Rupin did not know was that when he left, Sheila and Devraj were uncomfortable with each other alone. It seemed to work when Rupin was at home but as soon as they were alone, they could not find safe ground. Devraj would make his excuses and leave soon after Rupin had left.

As the months passed Rupin, Devraj and Sheila settled down to a comfortable co-existence. Devraj continued to visit and his discomfort with Sheila eased. Rupin had continued to watch them like a hawk and his suspicions festered internally and he became more determined to get even. Rupin did not want to confront Devraj until he had definite proof. Rupin was now becoming obsessed with revenge and spent most of his conscious hours planning and plotting revenge. This obsession in fact had become an escape from his real problems, his failing relationship with Sheila and his Klinefelter Syndrome medical condition.

Devraj on the other hand was trying earnestly to made amends for his deviant ways and seek salvation for his sexual attack on Buhle. His continued presence at Rupin and Sheila's house was a desperate and secret attempt to seek refuge from his self imposed incarceration and torture. There was not a day that passed in which Devraj did not put his head down in shame for his cruelty. Devraj wanted someday for Rupin to acknowledge what had happened that night in the sugar cane field and to condone his actions. He hung around Rupin like a naughty child waiting to be forgiven.

Sheila also became comfortable with Devraj's continued visits. She however was beginning to yearn for a child of her own. Deep down, Sheila knew that going to bed with Rupin for one night would not guarantee that she would fall pregnant so she wanted to double her chances. She planned and plotted on how best she could trick Devraj into fathering a child with her and seducing Rupin so that he would think it was his child. She had done it once so the concept was not foreign to her. In her mind she didn't particularly care who the father was, as long as she had a baby. The idea of also making love to Devraj appealed to her as she knew from past experience that he was a good lover. She had gone so long without sexual satisfaction that the more she thought about it the more determined she became to go along with her plans.

She could walk out of this marriage but then what kind of life could she live in a small town like this where divorced women were looked down upon. She enjoyed the envious looks she received from the other women because she was married to a Doctor. Being the Doctor's wife allowed her to be extravagant and she liked that too much to give it up. The perfect situation would be for her to trick Rupin into believing that he was the father of Devraj's child. She knew that making love to Rupin would be difficult as he did not seem to be interested in her sexually. Her plans had one flaw, the one thing that she did not know; Rupin had the Klinefelter Syndrome medical condition and that he could not father a child.

CHAPTER 15

Rupin was becoming more and more suspicious as the days passed. His wife was not her normal stand-offish self. She was constantly touching him and took every opportunity to brush against him. What really convinced him that something was amiss here was when she got up in the morning and showered whilst he was still in the bathroom shaving. He caught her in the mirror sneaking a look at him while she used her bath towel to slowly caress her wet and naked body while she dried her self up. He knew that this performance was for his benefit. This was most unusual as until now, she never even stirred in her sleep when he got up out of bed in the mornings. She however had not changed so drastically as to make him breakfast. That would have really shocked Rupin. He noticed that she dressed a little more seductively and her makeup was no longer subtle. What was also strange was that she would make small casual talk about his work and seemed to be interested in his emergency room duty schedules. Inquiries about his schedules were very subtle but Rupin registered the interest. If his suspicions had not sensitized him he would have missed those casual innocuous questions.

He also noticed that she seemed to be more alert of Devraj's visits and his schedules. Rupin knew that something was going down, but he could not figure out what it was. Rupin did not like being in the dark and not in control of the situation. He felt that he was the expert on Machiavellian endeavors and therefore should be in control and not be the one who is betrayed. With that in mind he decided to stage is own plan and flush out whatever was hatching in Sheila's head.

Devraj on the other hand was oblivious of the plotting and planning that was going on in Rupin's and Sheila's household. He continued to visit and enjoyed the additional attention he received from Sheila. He was unaware of Rupin's inquiring looks when ever Sheila was around him. Devraj's association with Rupin had given him some direction in following a career of his own. Rupin had arranged to find employment for Devraj as a data entry clerk in the records division at St Mary's Hospital where he worked. Rupin had done this so that he could keep an eye on Devraj during the day time hours. Rupin was becoming obsessed with his jealously as he believed that Sheila and Devraj were having an affair. He felt that his pain and anguish would be relieved if he could only catch them at it. Rupin was amazed at how clever the both of them were in hiding it from him as he had never caught them so far. Rupin knew that he would never rest until he caught them red handed. He did not want to approach them with his suspicions as he wanted the thrill of exposing them. Rupin was playing a destructive game that would only lead to disaster.

Little did Rupin know that Devraj was an innocent pawn in the devilish schemes of his wife, Sheila. Devraj, who once took advantage of an innocent soul, was now him self being taken advantage of with tragic consequences. Rupin continued with his diabolical plan, planting his own seeds of destruction.

******

The next few months passed without many incidents. Buhle's pregnancy was at full term and she became anxious about the delivery. It was common for the Sangoma to deliver the baby and she had become afraid of the Sangoma, especially after Themba had fought off Mapoza from attacking her. She had noticed the Sangoma looking at her strangely on several occasions.

Buhle grew closer to Themba and with some basic hand signings and drawings they were able to communicate and understand Mapoza's treachery. Buhle during a tender moment with Themba explained how she became pregnant. She left out the details to save him the pain and anguish of the attack by saying that she did not see the attacker as it was too dark in that sugar cane field.

Themba was enraged when he understood what had happened to Buhle and his love for her deepened. He made a promise to her that he would never let anything bad ever happen to her again as long as he lived. She put her head on his strong shoulders and felt her worries fade into the distant. She knew that between the two of them she would face any obstacles in front of them.

Mapoza had recovered from his beating although he walked with a limp. His broken leg had healed awkwardly since the broken bones were not set properly. Mapoza hated Themba intensely and stayed away from him and Buhle as he was afraid of him. He could not understand what had happened to Themba. He had returned so confident and strong. He concluded that the spirits on the riverbank had something to do with it. The Sangoma has told him that the bad spirits inhabited the river bank at night and Mapoza figured that Themba was possessed by one of those spirits. He knew that as long as Themba was alive he could not have Buhle so he planned to get rid of Themba. Mapoza was waiting for Themba to leave the village and then he would follow him. Mapoza managed to borrow a gun from one of his city friends and he knew that Themba was no match for that gun. All he had to do was to wait for the right opportunity.

The village was restless. Small groups of Zulu inhabitants gathered around the Sangoma. These Zulu inhabitants were considered the elders and the decision makers for the village. The Sangoma was priming these folks for the most drastic sacrifice to appease the spirits. She emphatically stated that the forefather's spirits were angry and the village would be destroyed if they did not act soon.

"The ancestral spirits are asking for blood, young human blood" she solemnly said in a deep voice. She let that sink in as the group digested the consequence of this drastic measure. Looking over at Buhle's hut, the Sangoma proceeded carefully.

"The young blood is being provided to us by the spirits and we need to give that life to the spirits to spare our lives and the village."

The group followed the Sangoma's gaze and saw her focus on Buhle who just stepped out of her hut. The group gasped at the realization that just hit them and they looked away. They knew that they had to support the Sangoma in this but this was so extreme. They would wait until the baby was born and then decide. After all with Themba being the father, they thought, the baby may be born as a mute. Then it would be much easier to justify the sacrifice. The Sangoma almost reading their minds, said'

"I created this problem by saving Themba when he was born. I should have allowed the spirits to take him away at birth. Now that mistake on my part has caused this unrest with our forefathers." Almost breathless the Sangoma continued,

"The spirits of our forefathers are giving us another chance. They are providing a second opportunity to appease them. The child that should not have lived many years ago is now giving us another child to make things right.'

CHAPTER 16

The Sangoma jolted upright in her bed. She thought she heard something, possibly a scream! She listened carefully but all she heard was the sound of the wind. She sat up in the darkness and listened, nothing stirred, not even the dogs that usually scrounge through the garbage looking for scraps of food. She lay down carefully so as to not disturb the shroud of eerie silence that blanketed the village. As she moved to a comfortable position on her straw bed on the floor, the myriad of beads around her neck made a rattling sound, like that of a rattle snake poised to strike. A storm was approaching and the wind was picking up screaming through the thatched roof of her hut.

She closed her eyes and hoped the storm would pass while she slept. The wind continued to pick up and a loose piece of metal sheeting went skating across the front of her hut, crashing with some clay pots. The dark sky flashed as lightning bolts tore through it, temporarily illuminating in the sky a canvas of tormented souls searching for salvation. The Sangoma opened her eyes in anticipation of the thunder boom that usually follows a flash of lightning. She waited and waited; nothing. Dead silence prevailed. And then it came, a gut wrenching spasm in her gut. The Sangoma bolted up and doubled over in pain, a contraction of her lower abdomen muscles so severe that it brought tears to her eyes. She knew immediately what she had to do. It was always like this whenever one of the women was going into labor and she needed to be there. It was usually a mild twitching that summoned her, but this was intense, this was no ordinary birth.

The lightning lit up the sky casting ghostly images in all directions as the Sangoma hurriedly made her way to Buhle's hut. The wind tore at the edges of the thatched roofs of the huts, trying desperately to get inside while the inhabitants pulled their blankets and bed covers a little tighter over themselves. The Sangoma dared to steal a glance at the turbulent sky, and even she was worried. Arriving at Buhle's hut, the Sangoma without announcing her presence pushed open the door and entered.

A lantern on the table dimly illuminated the interior of the hut. The flame in the lantern danced to some frenzied tempo, casting lurking shadows all around the walls of the hut. The shadows cast on the walls seemed to fill the room like an audience at a melancholy opera. At center stage sprawled on her simple straw bed, lay Buhle, her flimsy clothing clinging to her sweat drenched body. Themba was kneeling at her side and cradling her head in his lap. He was terrified at what was happening to Buhle as he did not understand or ever witness the birth of a baby. He tried on several occasions to fetch help from the Sangoma but Buhle held on to him tightly and begged him not to leave her. Her fingernails dug so deeply into his flesh that it broke the skin in some places and drew blood. Themba made no attempt to abandon her and tolerated the pain. Against his better judgment he stayed to comfort her. Themba was very relieved when the Sangoma burst into the hut but Buhle did not share that feeling. She was apprehensive and had an ominous premonition that her baby was in danger.

The Sangoma took one look at a Buhle and knew that it was time to deliver the baby. She ordered Themba out of the room and asked him to boil some water. Themba tore himself loose from Buhle knowing full well that the Sangoma had work to do and that men were precluded from these events. Buhle reached for Themba begging him not to leave her alone with the Sangoma but she was too weak to hold on. Before she knew it, Themba had left the room to do his chores and she was left alone looking into the bright whites of the eyes of the Sangoma. A sense of dread gripped her as another intense contraction rippled down her lower back and put its iron clad arms around her lower abdomen and squeezed. Buhle involuntarily raised her upper body in response to the pain and her thrashing hands grabbed the Sangoma's beads and ripped it off her shoulders scattering the beads in all directions onto the hut floor. Buhle screamed in agony, a blood curdling scream that stopped Themba in his tracks outside the hut.

Themba was not sure what he should do, should he go in and help Buhle or go and boil the water as he was told to do. He walked in circles vacillating between rushing in to help Buhle or boiling water for her. With much trepidation he chose to boil some water and leave the women to deal with the birthing process. He remembered that someone once told him that there was a lot of screaming when a baby was born and it was best for the men folk to leave and let the women deal with it. This notion stripped the guilt from him as he picked up a container to fetch water from the river.

Buhle collapsed from sheer exhaustion as the contraction relaxed its vice like grip. She felt a wave of drowsiness pass over her and she tried desperately to stay awake. As she drifted off for a much needed rest she remembered seeing the Sangoma examine her to see how far along she was. The bed on the floor that Buhle lay on was soaked with her blood. Buhle was bleeding profusely and although the Sangoma noticed this dangerous condition she ignored it and concentrated on the baby's head that was starting to crown at the entrance of the birth canal. The Sangoma was perturbed at the sight of the baby's head. The head seemed to have a full crop of black hair, which was unlike that of a Zulu baby. A Zulu baby was usually born with a fine short crop of curly hair or with little or no hair at all. This baby had a thick growth of hair and the hair was fine and straight.

The Sangoma did not like what she was seeing and it was becoming more obvious to her that this baby should be sacrificed to appease the spirits. The Sangoma was so preoccupied with her thoughts that she did not notice Buhle open her eyes as another contraction prepared a toboggan slide down her muscles, twisting and turning as it peaked at the base of her spine. Buhle held her breath and some basic instinct urged her to push downwards with every muscle in her body. She felt the entrance of her birth canal stretch and an intense burning sensation radiated between her legs. She felt the head pass through the entrance of the birth canal and she felt a cooling sensation return as the entrance of the birth canal relaxed. Buhle sucked in cool fresh air and collapsed onto her bed exhausted and weak. The break was short lived as another contraction swelled and rose like a tsunami charging down her lower back with a second wave following close behind. Charged with the basic instinct to procreate Buhle pushed with all her might and although she could feel her muscles tear at the base , she did not care, she pushed again, this time harder than the first until she felt the baby's shoulder exit her body. And then she collapsed with exhaustion. The lightning outside breaking through the clouds, zigzagged across the sky, its episiotomy tearing the clouds apart ushered the baby into the hands of the Sangoma.

The Sangoma stared at the baby, not believing what she saw. The baby did not look like a Zulu baby. The baby resembled that of a baby belonging to the Indians who lived in the nearby town. Even the skin color was all wrong. The baby was fair skinned and not dark skinned as a Zulu baby would have been. The Sangoma was so disturbed by this revelation that she forgot to look at the sex of the baby. Shaking herself loose from her state of shock she looked at the baby and discovered that the baby was a female. The Sangoma knew that she had to get the baby away from Buhle before she awoke. The Sangoma quickly cut the umbilical cord and cleaned the baby's face and cleared its nose and mouth so that the baby could breathe.

Without much prompting the baby cried weakly. It was a weak cry but was enough to wake Buhle from her coma induced sleep. By this time the Sangoma had the baby wrapped in a small cloth and was turning to leave the hut. Buhle tried to get up and stop her from taking her baby away from her but she was too weak to get up. She tried to call out for help but all that came out from her parched throat was a raspy whisper. She was losing her baby and there was nothing she could do to stop it.

CHAPTER 17

With the newly born baby wrapped in the cloth the Sangoma watched with disgust Buhle's feeble attempt to stop her. Even as she stood there she saw Buhle arch her back as another contraction racked her body, this time expelling the after birth. The Sangoma could see that Buhle had lost a lot of blood and she needed attention, but her priority now was not Buhle's health but was to get the baby away. She was now convinced more than ever that the spirits of her forefathers were angry and needed to be appeased, why else would they send a baby looking like this. The elders in the village would surely support her now when they see what this baby looked like and that combined with the rage in the skies during the birth would leave no doubt in their minds.

Taking one last look at the feeble mother, the Sangoma with the baby held close against her chest, stepped out of the hut and almost bumped into a dark figure standing in her path. Startled, she looked up into the smiling face of Themba who had his hands stretched out to accept the baby. The Sangoma was speechless, she had no control over Themba now, especially since, over the last few months he had matured into a formidable young man. Grimacing and biting her lower lip she handed the baby to Themba. She then stepped around him and without turning back she hurriedly departed against the dying wind.

Themba took the baby into the hut and kneeling down placed the baby into Buhle's eager outstretched arms. The baby sensing the mother's breast turned her head to ravenously feed. Themba watched the mother and child with awe. He did not notice the difference in the baby's appearance and neither did the mother. Both of them embraced each other allowing the baby's presence to consume them.

The Sangoma summoned the elders to her hut and waited impatiently for them to assemble. The elders filed into the hut looking concerned with the decision that had to be made. They had barely entered the hut when the Sangoma exploded with rage. She described in detail the aberration she witnessed and the need to appease the spirits of their forefathers. The Sangoma ranted and raved and the bewildered elders stood around her shuffling their feet uncomfortably. Pounding the air with her fist the Sangoma's outburst continued.

"How can a baby looking so different from us be born to Buhle and Themba?" She looked at each one of them in turn as if she expected them to know the answer.

"This is a trick played on us by the spirits of our forefathers. We cannot let this baby grow up in our village." She paused for acknowledgement but got none. The elders were still trying to digest this situation. One of them ventured to ask,

"Is the baby deformed in anyway, have the spirits cursed her like they cursed Themba by taking away his voice and mind?" The Sangoma looked at the elder with fiery eyes. She threw up her arms with impatience as the elder stepped back expecting to be struck.

"Yes that baby is deformed. She has straight black hair, Lots of it. She has skin color like muddy water and strange nose, narrow with thin lips. She is not normal like us." She glared at them for reaction but was getting dumb founded looks; she continued,

"Those eyes, when you look at them, they are like bottomless wells. And the spirits seem to lurk in them". The Sangoma saying this threw her hands up in frustration,

"And I would have had the baby with me if Themba had not come. He is also possessed by the spirits, making those strange hand signs at Buhle. The spirits are working through him and that is why the baby looks like that. He made that baby". Now the Sangoma was drained and she sat down on a wooden stool. For effect, she put her head in her hands and rocked back and forth chanting. The remaining beads around her shoulders rattling like maracas in a voodoo ritual dance. Ensuring that control does not pass to the elders, she got up after a few minutes and calmly said,

"Just think what would happen in our village if we allow this child to grow up with our children. She will be different and she will be mocked by the others. There will be no peace again in our village". This invoked some reaction from the elders, for now she was talking about their children and grandchildren. Discovering an opening that she could take advantage off, she continued,

"What if she has evil spirits in her, she would be amongst our children and make them sick or even kill the ones that tease her".

Now she had gotten through to them as they were visibly affected by this possibility. They stood around nodding to each other while the Sangoma wringed her bony hands in victory. Taking advantage of the momentum she gained, the Sangoma said,

"At sunrise tomorrow, we will offer our sacrifice to our forefathers and ask for peace to return to our village. The four of you go to Buhle's hut and tell her that you will come at sunrise tomorrow to give the baby a bath."

The four elders shifted nervously as they did not expect to actually be involved in this ceremony. The Sangoma quick to sense the sudden hesitation followed through with,

"At sunrise tomorrow, when you get there to give the baby a bath, ask Themba to fetch some water from the river and heat it up for the baby's bath. He will be very willing as Buhle cannot get out of her bed to bath the baby and the baby will need a bath"

The Sangoma saw some relief come to their faces and so she gently prodded on.

"When you see Themba leave, two of you attend to Buhle's condition and the other two should bring the baby to me". Seeing that this plan was doable to them they nodded in agreement. The Sangoma continued with the plan to further ease their fears.

"I will prepare the place for the sacrifice, it will be quick; the spirits will be pleased. I will explain all of this to Buhle and Themba when it is over".

The Sangoma did not want to think about how she would do it but she knew she would call on the spirits to help her with that task. The Sangoma sat down again and began to chant. Using a stick with a brush at its end she fanned the small incense pot. The scented smoke billowed into the hut stinging and bringing tears to the eyes of the elders. They looked at the Sangoma for approval to leave but she was in a trance, chanting to the spirits, her white painted face ashen in appearance with only the whites of her eyes showing through half closed eyelids. They quickly turned on their heels and scrambled out of the hut.

Mapoza smiled for the first time after a long time. He saw the elders leave in a hurry and chuckled. He had heard every word from his hiding place outside the hut. He knew something was going on when he heard his mother the Sangoma rounding up the elders so early in the morning. He sneaked up to the Sangoma's hut and took in every word. He was shocked to hear about the baby, but then he knew nothing good would come out of Themba anyway. He was pleased, for he had a diabolical plan. He would follow Themba at a safe distance to the river the next morning. When Themba bent over at the river's edge to fill water into the container, he would shoot him and let the river take the body away. Mapoza had decided that he would not get close to Themba, or even let him know that he was being stalked. There was something supernatural about Themba and Mapoza did not want to find out what it was. The weight of the gun in his pocket comforted him and as he got up to leave he patted his pocket and grinned. This was the best day of his life.

CHAPTER 18

Two of the elders from the umuzi stopped over at Buhle's hut to offer to bathe the baby. Buhle and Themba were extremely grateful for the help as Buhle was very weak from the blood loss and could not care for the baby. The elders looked at each other knowingly when they saw the baby and were convinced that the Sangoma was right. This baby did not belong in the umuzi with their children.

These elder women however were not cruel and they genuinely cared for Buhle. Whilst they were there they asked Themba to fetch some hot water while one prepared to bathe and care for Buhle whilst the other cleaned the baby and made her comfortable. When they were done they prepared some food for Buhle and fed her. They then cleaned up the hut and made Buhle comfortable and promised to stop by later to help out again. With tears in their eyes and heavy hearts they left the hut wishing that they did not have to carry out their ominous plan the next morning.

Themba spent most of the day fussing over Buhle and the baby. He was enjoying this new role and could not be happier. He loved the baby and she slept in his arms for most of the day. Buhle faded in an out of sleep and struggled to stay awake to let the baby feed. Buhle had an uncanny feeling that something was amiss. She caught a glimpse of the elders looking at the baby and then at each other and their expression on their face sent warning signals to her. She was not sure whether she had imagined it or not. She turned to Themba and the look on his face holding the baby comforted her and her fears dissolved into sheer bliss.

As the day passed into evening there was a growing tension in the umuzi. Themba's senses were heightened and he was becoming more and more concerned as the hours passed. As the ominous darkness slowly strangled the daylight, Themba became uneasy. The darkness always exaggerated the situation and to add to his worries Themba sensed that Buhle was not doing well. She was very pale and was fading in and out of consciousness. All his senses were nagging him to seek medical assistance from the modern White man's medicine. He had lost confidence in the

Sangoma's methods. What Themba was not aware of was that Buhle had developed a condition of "Amniotic Fluid Embolism" brought about by the difficult birth and the blood loss. A volume of amniotic fluid had entered her blood stream and had traveled to her lungs causing the arteries in her lungs to constrict. The constriction was causing her to have rapid heart beats and irregular heart rhythm. She was going into shock. This was serious and without help she might suffer cardiac arrest and possibly die from this condition.

Themba was now becoming desperate and he needed to get some help. As he racked his brain looking for some salvation, two of the elders stopped by to check on Buhle and the baby. Stepping into the hut, they promptly asked Themba to leave as they wanted to wash Buhle and the baby. Themba was thankful for the relief but hated to leave Buhle. He tried to communicate to the elders that Buhle needed medical attention but they did not understand his sign language and concluded that he too was possessed. Frustrated for not being able to communicate, he left the hut and sat on the wooden bench outside the hut.

Having the handicap of not being able to talk had its advantages because in Themba's situation his other senses had become acute especially his hearing. From the wooden bench outside the hut Themba could hear the elders talk amongst themselves. The fact that Themba could not talk tended to lull them into the false notion that he also could not hear and therefore they were not careful on what they said. They also saw that Buhle was sleeping deeply and this made them even more careless in what they said. One elder said to the other,

"It is good that the baby is strong and is doing well because the spirits of our forefathers would not want us to send a sick baby to them". The other elder responded,

"This is a terrible thing. Our umuzi is in so much of pain. All should be back in harmony after tomorrow morning"

Although they did not outline clearly what was going to happen Themba was able to piece together what was going to happen the next morning. He knew what the Sangoma was planning and although it was a warm evening, he shivered from the thought. After a short while the elders made their exit after feeding the baby. They were visibly concerned on what was going to happen the next morning.

When they left Themba went back into the hut and tried to wake Buhle from her semi-conscious state. Even now she looked paler than before and shivered in the warm evening air. The baby cried and Themba immediately picked her up and gently rocked her to pacify her. The sound of the baby's cry plunged deeply into Buhle's core and she fluttered her eyelids and struggled to grasp her conscious world. Themba took advantage of this moment of coherence and signed to her that the baby was in danger and he needed to hide her away from the Sangoma. It did not surprise Buhle as she struggled to stay awake; she would expect that the Sangoma would resort to devious acts. She whispered to him,

"Themba, you are the only one I can trust to help my baby". Sobbing openly she continued between gasps,

"There is an Indian doctor who works at St Mary's Hospital across the sugar cane field on the main road." Themba was confused but Buhle continued struggling to say awake,

"Take my baby to him and leave her there. He will take care of her. I will wait for you to return, no matter how long it takes for you to get back". Buhle did not know why she had said that, she seemed to have a sickening premonition that they may never see each other again. Themba was frozen; he could not command his body to move. The task ahead of him was so daunting that he was afraid that he would not accomplish it. He was too afraid that he would fail, and most importantly he would fail Buhle. Tears from Themba's eyes rolled down his cheeks as he bit his lips and looked at Buhle, his eyes pleading with her to not trust him with such a precious task. Buhle knew that for her baby's sake she needed to muster every ounce of energy and encourage Themba to be strong. With all her might she sat up and reached for Themba, the baby gently squeezed between them.

She whispered in his ears, her tears on her wet cheeks mixing with his,

"Themba, you are the guardian angel for our precious daughter. You must save her. Please keep her safe and take her when all the people in the umuzi are gone to bed. You will know this Indian Doctor when you see him; he has a dark scar on the side of his face". With a last gasp she said,

"He is not the father of this child but he knows who is and he will do the right thing". And with that she fell back onto the bed, tears streaming down her cheeks. She reached for the baby but her hands fell short as she faded into unconsciousness. With barely an audible whisper she said'

"Themba go safely and come back to me, I will wait for you", and with that she was sucked helplessly into the abyss.

Themba sat beside Buhle, the baby cradled in his arms and cried as he rocked back and forth. Some time had past and the umuzi slowly settled down for the night. Themba wrapped the baby tightly and as he got up to leave for his impossible mission, he gently kissed Buhle on her lips. He found that she was cold and clammy and that made him uncomfortable. He decided that he would first take the baby to safety and then he would return to her and also carry her to the hospital.

Mapoza was too excited to sleep. Finally he would have his revenge. Mapoza decided to spend this night in Themba's secret hiding place in the tree. He smiled as he mounted that tree as it was such a convenient spot. He cynically thanked Themba for the best view he could possibly have over Buhle's hut. As he sat there replaying in his mind what he would do, he saw movement at Buhle's hut. He rubbed his eyes for he could not believe what he was seeing; Themba was quietly leaving the hut with the baby.

Mapoza waiting for a few seconds and then quietly climbed down the tree. When he got to the bottom he reached into his pocket and drew the gun. He held it to his cheeks and the cool feel of the steel against his skin was comforting. He said to himself, plans have changed but the outcome will be the same. He held the gun firmly in the palm of his hands and carefully followed Themba at a safe distance into the sugar cane field.

CHAPTER 19

Rupin decided to fake a trip to a medical conference. He made an entry in his daily planner for an overnight trip to Durban for the following week. He labeled the entry as a one day medical conference. He carefully placed the planner in his briefcase and left it within plain view in his office. He knew that Sheila had regularly looked through his planner before, because he found the orientation of the planner in his briefcase to be different to the way he placed it. He grinned to himself as he thought on how predictable she was.

The day of his fake conference arrived and Sheila was full of nervous energy. She had attempted that previous night to seduce him but it was a failure before it even began. Rupin was preoccupied with his planning and so consumed with his jealousy that he was oblivious to her advances. Sheila also was preoccupied and anxious and made a half hearted attempt at getting his attention. The first part of her plan had failed miserably and she was determined not to let the second part fail too. Rupin had provided enough information to Sheila so that she knew that he was planning to stay overnight in Durban but made sure that he kept other details fairly vague. Durban was a fairly large city on the east coast of South Africa about hundred miles away from his home.

He also made sure that Devraj knew that he was leaving and he was expecting to see his eyes light up with the prospect of getting together with Sheila for the night. Rupin was puzzled when instead of showing excitement, Devraj was disappointed. Rupin concluded that Devraj was very good at how he showed his emotions. This made Rupin even more determined to catch them in the act. His elusive victory was becoming more priceless. Rupin had no time for speculations at this time. He had to make arrangements for his fake business trip and pick up a rental car. He wanted a rental car for two reasons; one to lend credibility to his elaborate plan and the other reason was to make him inconspicuous as he executed his plan.

That evening Rupin drove his rental car into his neighborhood and found a spot that concealed the car from the view of his house. He came prepared with food and coffee for the long wait ahead of him, but he had a feeling that he would not have to wait long. From his car he could see his driveway that led up to his house and hoped that he could hear what happens inside. He was like a kid with a forbidden task at hand; he was energized at this mission. He sat in his rental car with his binoculars and played through his mind what he would do when he caught them. He was sure that he would catch them in a compromising position and then, he stopped. Then what? He sat back in the car seat and asked the question; then what? Thoughts came flooding back to him as he tried desperately to separate the different strains of emotions he harbored over the last year. He knew that he did not want to get rid of Sheila from his life and neither did he want to get rid of Devraj. So what did he want out of the plan? The word emerged from his inner core; control.

He wanted control. He wanted to be in charge of Sheila and Devraj. He wanted them to grovel at his feet and beg for mercy. He had been taken advantage of by Sheila and Devraj and they had deceived him and they should pay. Yes, he pounded on the steering wheel, he was wronged and they had to pay. He would hold their deception over their head and like slaves to a king he would rule. His anger subsided to a calm menacing demure as he justified his actions. His mind went back to the sugar cane field, nine months ago and he hated Devraj for what was done to that Zulu girl. But he hated Devraj even more for making him an accessory to such a travesty; how dare he put him in such a difficult situation. In his twisted reasoning, Rupin placed all the blame on Devraj and doing so absolved himself of any blame for letting it happen. Rupin relaxed his shoulders and sucked in a breath as he reaffirmed his mission to get revenge. He needed to stay cool and not ruin his carefully laid out plans.

Sheila could not settle down this evening. She confirmed that Rupin had left for the evening by calling his office and the rental car pickup confirmed his absence. It was close to midnight and she had changed her outfit several times as she waited for Devraj to make his customary visit. As the evening dragged on and after several outfit changes she came to the conclusion that Devraj was not going to make his customary evening visit. She hated him for it, for being so righteous, for being so spineless. She was not going to let this opportunity slip away; she was going to take charge.

She went to the phone in the hallway and called Devraj. After several persistent rings a sleepy voice answered'

"Hello". Sheila recognized Devraj's voice and she fumed. The bastard was sleeping and here she was expecting him to come over. Off course she had not asked him to come over, she just expected him to come. After all men were creatures of habit, she reflected and this man is no different. She asked herself why she even bothered, he was only good for one thing and that was to father her child. Feigning anguish in her voice she pleaded'

"Devraj, I am scared, please come over, I need your help, please please, I don't feel good". Devraj was wide awake now and tried to cut in on her pleading to calm her down. He wanted to know what the problem was but before he could ask she put the phone back on its cradle. He promptly called her back but she deliberately did not answer. She looked at her watch and said to her self "in ten minutes, he will be at the front door". And in a fairly inaudible voice, she said to no one in particular, "men are so pliable". She had five minutes to change into something more comfortable.

As predicted Devraj, concerned for Sheila's well being came up to the front door and before he could pound on it, Sheila opened the door and stood there in a flimsy negligee. Devraj was breathing heavily having rushed over, concerned for Sheila. He glared at her trying to catch his breath and as he focused he could not believe what he was seeing. Sheila smiled seductively and invited him in. Devraj was too shocked to question so he followed her in like a lamb to the slaughter. Sheila turned on her heels and using the sole of her foot she pushed the door closed.

Rupin almost jumped in his seat when he saw Devraj's car come up the driveway to his house. The blood rushed to his head in anticipation; he pounded the steering wheel; he knew he was right. Now was his chance to catch them red handed. He was too excited to think, but he knew that he needed to wait for a while to let them get comfortable. He just did not know how he would be able to sit in his car, even for a minute. Rupin sat in his rental car, drumming his fingers on the dashboard of the car and waited. He forced himself to wait although every muscle in his body was poised to move. He was already playing out his entry scene in his mind and kept telling himself that he was right. He could taste the revenge in his mouth and it was sweet.

CHAPTER 20

Devraj was quick to compose himself and demanded an explanation. He was angry because her call to him had worried him and he had recklessly driven at dangerously high speeds to come over to help her only to be confronted by this. He was too angry to be turned on by her or for that matter by any other female at this time. Sheila touched his face to calm him down and softly whispered in his ear,

"We are alone. Rupin is gone for the night. It has been so long". Devraj pushed her away from him and with controlled anger he said,

"Go and cover yourself. You have misjudged me; I am not going to disrespect Rupin, he is my friend". Sheila drew a breath in and stepped back, she had never been rejected before and it did not feel good. The blood rose to her cheeks and a wave of anger spread over her. She wanted to lash out at Devraj but decided not to, there was still a chance that she would be able to win him over. She had misjudged him over the last year as she had always thought that he visited Rupin because he was secretly in love with her and wanted to be around her. She had enjoyed that notion over that time and now her self esteem and pride had taken a dive.

She went into the bathroom and grabbed a gown and put it on. When she got back Devraj was at the front door. He calmly said,

"Go ahead and lock up for the night and we would not mention this incident again". With that he walked out leaving Sheila speechless.

******

Johan Botha came on duty at ten o'clock in the evening. He walked into the locker room of the South African Police Station in Harding to change into his police uniform. As he walked in he saw his partner Piet Coetzee standing next to his locker putting on his kaki police shirt. As he approached Piet he slapped him on the back and almost sent him flying into the locker. Piet did not have to turn around to know who it was and he was afraid that it was going to be one of those nights; Johan was overly caffeinated. Piet was a quiet resentful man in his mid twenties. The highly energetic Johan was assigned to be his partner so that he could act as a calming influence on him.

Johan had returned from active duty, serving at the border patrol in Angola and he was anxious for more action. There were a lot of politically motivated uprisings and violence in the area and the Police force was strengthened to maintain and contain any unrests. This environment excited Johan for he wanted action and was trigger happy. There was a lot of tension in the Black Homelands especially in this area, ever since the White South African Government had issued the Afrikaans Medium Decree. This decree mandated that all schools use the Afrikaans language as the medium for instruction in the class room. There were uprisings in many schools with the children protesting this law. This law angered the students since the Black languages were not allowed as the medium for instructions in the classroom.

This policy was deeply unpopular, since Afrikaans was regarded by some in the area as the language of the oppressor. In April of nineteen seventy six, students at Orlando West Junior School and other schools in Soweto went on strike, refusing to go to school. The students organized a mass rally which turned violent. Police killed over twenty students, which triggered widespread violence throughout South Africa. It is believed the death toll rose to over two hundred. The tension in the country was further aggravated by the death of Steve Biko, founder and martyr of the Black Consciousness movement in South Africa. He was a prominent advocate for freedom from White Government oppression.

Johan loved this time as it gave him immense power and freedom of action to shoot any person he felt that was a threat for a political uprising. He had the guns and the Blacks did not; that made him feel in total control. For Johan, being in the armed forces at this time was a thrill and he enjoyed the night shift as it provided an element of danger for him. At the same time any errors in judgment on his part could easily be justified by the cover of darkness.

Piet tolerated Johan but wished that he was not so intense. Piet just wanted a quiet shift so he could go home to his wife and two kids in the morning. Piet hated being on the late night shift as he was always concerned about his family's safety. When Piet lived in Johannesburg his house was broken into and his family terrorized by a couple of Black South African young men. Piet was angry and requested a transfer to

Harding, Natal. Harding was located in a rural area and he expected that it would be safer here than living in a large city like Johannesburg. Although he never had reason to be alarmed about the safety in Harding, Piet was nervous about leaving his family alone at night. His experiences in Johannesburg had made Piet resentful of the South African Black people and he did not have much empathy for their lives.

Piet dressed into his kaki uniform and put his pen in his shirt pocket. Seeing that pen in Piet's shirt pocket, Johan recalled the evening that a mute Black man reached for that pen. Johan could clearly see in his mind's eye the scene that played out at the roadside. Johan pointed at the pen in Piet's pocket and as he did he made a squealing sound, imitating the mute they encountered that night several months ago. He then hobbled around the locker room holding his head feigning pain and all the while hissing and squealing for mercy. The scene played out in the locker room was tragic in its consequence but the way Johan acted it out brought a smile to Piet's face and they both left the locker room together laughing as they headed out to their police van to tackle their night patrol.

Because of the increased tension in the area each of the patrol vans were equipped with a, Deutsche Schaferhund more commonly known as an Alsatian dog. These dogs are a breed of German Sheppard especially trained as police guard dogs. These dogs were intelligent and extremely faithful to their handlers and when agitated they terrified the bystanders with their long nose and a set of large incisors. In fact most folks were more afraid of the Alsatian on the leash than the gun in the policeman's holster. The Alsatian was already in the caged compartment at the back of the police van and as Johan came up to the vehicle he pounded on the side panel of the van to startle the sleeping dog. The dog bolted upright and growled at Johan but stopped as soon as he recognized Piet at Johan's side. Johan laughed at this show of dominance and got into the drivers seat with Piet sliding into the passenger seat. The spinning tires on the gravel dirt sent the police van hurtling forward into the night in a cloud of dust, towards the sugar cane fields.

Their first stop was at St Mary's Hospital emergency room. This was a good starting place to gauge the level of unrest amongst the Zulu inhabitants. Invariably the seriously injured freedom fighters would be transported there, having been involved in some confrontation or the other.

Johan enjoyed strutting through the emergency room and the adjoining hospital hallways with his automatic rifle in one hand and the other at the ready on his holster. The frightened looks on the predominantly Black patients waiting for attention just made him walk taller.

What Johan did not know was that this night was going to be different. He would get all the action he craved for and more, ending in life long tragic consequences.

CHAPTER 21

The full moon with its mournful light lit up the sugar cane field like an opera stage in Bellini's lyric tragedy "Norma". The strong breeze singing through the sugar cane reeds augmented the scene, filling the air with the aria, "Casta diva" a bel canto soprano of the 19th century. A masterpiece performance was soon to be acted to its tragic end by brother and half brother.

Themba's senses heightened as he entered the swaying sugar cane field. For the first time he felt vulnerable, his inability to talk weighing him down in this outside world. Carrying the baby had incapacitated his ability to communicate by signing and so here he was; not knowing exactly were he was going to and not being able to ask for help. The foremost burden of responsibility he endured even before his own life was that of the safety of the baby. He did not want to fail Buhle. Themba was unaware that Mapoza was following him since the cunning hunter was stalking Themba by watching the protesting sugar cane stalks thrashing in the path of his prey. Mapoza wanted Themba to be in the thick of the field before he would close in on him.

Themba was not sure of the way to the hospital but he knew his way to the main road and from there he would figure how to get to the hospital. There would be signs posted on the road and he would follow its direction. The baby was impervious to all the stress around her and was sleeping comfortably in Themba's arms. Themba was surprised when the sugar cane field suddenly opened into the side of a deserted road. As he cautiously stepped onto the road to figure which direction he should go, he noticed approaching headlights speeding towards him. He stood rooted to the spot like the proverbial deer in headlights, his right hand shielding his eyes from the brightness.

The vehicle braked hard, its squealing tires grabbed the elusive road surface for support. The vehicle back end spun half way around before the vehicle ground to a stop, the dust of the road finally catching up to it. Themba was aware that he was holding his breath and exhaled slowly.

Themba squinted his eyes to try and make out the two figures that had disembarked and were striding towards him. With the dust swirling around the vehicle and figures walking in the dust illuminated by the strong headlight beams, the scene looked like aliens walking away from a space ship. And then he heard it, a squealing sound imitating a pig came from one of the figures and then uncontrolled laughter. As Johan and Piet got closer, laughing uncontrollably, Themba saw the pen in the shirt pocket of one of the policemen. His heart sank as he remembered the last time he saw that pen.

Themba felt that this was not the time for negotiations or explanations. Without any warning, he turned around and sprinted into the sugar cane field holding the baby close to his chest. He heard a warning from one of the policemen,

"Stop kaffir, or I will shoot you, this is the police". Themba ignored the warning as a bullet from a gun shot whizzed past him. Themba dove back into the sugar cane field and bolted through it, protecting the baby from being hit by the sugar cane stalks that sprung back.

Johan called out to Piet as he pulled out his baton and sprinted to the sugar cane field.

"It is the Black mute again. It looks like he stole something and he is hiding it in a blanket. Wait here I will get him, he is mine".

With that he cut through the sugar cane field following the sound of thrashing sugar cane stalks. It suddenly got quiet and Johan tensed as he stopped to listen. He then cautiously made his way through the field in the direction that he thought he had heard his suspect run. He cursed himself for not bringing a flash light with him from the police van. Johan was still trying to orient himself when felt the blow to his face and chest before he even saw the closed fisted hand that hit him. Johan was struck with such a force that he was first lifted off his feet before being thrown back in his tracks. He hit the ground hard with his back, the breath knocked out of him.

Instinctively he reached for his holstered gun and fired at the dark figure looming over him. Themba reeled backwards with the impact of the bullet trying to keep his balance but still holding on to the baby. Johan lay on the ground for a moment gasping for air and then like a trained fighter he rolled over and sprung to his feet. As he turned ready for action he found that Themba having recovered slightly was almost on top of him. Themba's strong hand gripped Johan's gun hand and tried to wrestle it out of him. They fought for possession of the gun with Johan's finger pressed against the trigger. The gun recoiled as it fired and Johan momentarily released his grip losing the gun to his attacker.

Themba stood upright with Johan's gun in hand as Piet's flashlight beam traced his outline and focused on his face. Piet drew his gun but before he could fire, Themba's knees buckled and he slowly sank to the ground but kept the baby safe in his arms. The baby's blanket slowly soaking up the blood from Themba's bleeding wound. Johan was still standing and with shaky legs he turned to Piet and with a raspy voice said,

"The kaffir shot me" and then smiling to himself he said "but I got the bastard". As the last words trailed into a whisper he spun on his legs as they gave way and slumped to the ground like a rag doll.

Mapoza with his gun still in hand stood up from his crouched position in a nearby spot in the sugar cane field. He saw the whole scene play out in front of him but was too scared to intervene. He was so shocked to see a person actually being shot and especially it being Themba that he stood up oblivious to the fact that there was still another policeman on the scene. Mapoza had always thought of himself as a rough and tough freedom fighter but had never witnessed a man being shot. This violence shocked him. Piet saw him rise from the ground and instinctively fired his gun in the general direction of the movement. The shot went wild. The gun shot brought Mapoza back to reality and he turned and bolted through the sugar cane being narrowly missed by one of the two bullets that were fired at him.

Considering the circumstances, Piet was calm. He hated that the Blacks wanted to take over the country. He believed in the apartheid system and believed that the Blacks had their homelands and they should stay there. It was time to show these people who really is in charge. Piet quickly knelt down and felt for a pulse on Johan's neck. Piet dropped his head in sorrow as he realized that Johan was dead; another one of his comrades lost to these people. Piet raised his radio to his mouth and called the riot squad for assistance. He gave his location and details of the uprising and then clipped his radio microphone to his shoulder harness.

As he headed back to his van to get his Alsatian dog, he quickly focused the flashlight beam on Themba and noticed the blood soaked blanket with the baby wrapped inside it. With his boots he kicked the man on the ground but go no response. He looked at his boot carefully to make sure that it did not have any blood on it and as he walked away he reported into his radio'

"Johan was shot dead by an armed Zulu gang. Johan had fought like a true Afrikaaner for his country. He single handily fought off the gang and killed one of them." He continued almost mechanically,

"We need to round up this lot and quell the uprising before it gets out of hand like in the big cities. I am going to get my Alsatian and go after them, please come quickly".

Getting closer to his police van he remembered the baby in the blood soaked blanket. Needing to call it in, he raised his radio to his mouth and said,

"Oh by the way a Black baby was also killed in the struggle."

CHAPTER 22

Rupin decided it was time to confront Sheila and Devraj. As he reached for the ignition switch he saw several riot vehicles race down the road with horns blazing and lights flashing. These vehicles were usually called out to control riots and political uprisings. Following closely were several ambulances also rushing to some crises situation. As these vehicles passed him his pager urgently beeped with a code he dreaded to see. It was a predetermined code that urgently requested all medical personnel to report for duty at the emergency room. Rupin was a dedicated doctor and as much as he had other matters to attend to he knew that he had to go to the hospital to fulfill his duty as a doctor. There was obviously a serious situation developing and his help was needed.

Piet saw the riot vehicles arrive and about twenty men from each vehicle disembarked fully equipped with riot gear. In an instant there was a hive of activity along this quiet road. Alsatian dogs were straining against their leashes barking and growling at some unknown assailant urging their handlers to let them go. Piet bristled with pride at the show of force. He wanted a quiet night but that kaffir changed it all by killing his partner and now the whole village would pay the price.

Commander Villiers came over to Piet and they discussed the situation. After strategizing for a few minutes the commander barked out some orders in Afrikaans and the riot squad sprung into action. They fanned out, some pulled by the over anxious dogs whilst others slashed at the sugar cane stalks, destroying the field as they converged on the village.

Mapoza heard the dogs and he broke out in a sweat. This was not good; he could feel it in the pit of his stomach. This was one problem even the Sangoma could not help him with. If he was thinking straight he would have headed for the river and away from the village. He stood a better chance of losing them in the water. The dogs would lose the scent and he would make it across the river safely. But he was not thinking clearly, he was in survival mode. As he ran towards the village he saw Buhle's hut and darted for it.

Two Indian emergency crew members went to fetch Johan's body from the sugar cane field. They were thankful that they were not involved in the mayhem that was soon to erupt across the hill. When they got to Johan's body they set the stretcher down and noticed Themba lying on the ground. The bright lights that the riot squad set up also illuminated this tragic scene and they saw the baby in the blood soaked blanket. The one that was obviously the leader said to his assistant,

"Go back to the truck and bring two body bags. See if you can get a small one for the baby. With all that blood lost, that baby did not stand a chance, the poor thing so little had lived for such a short time"

Themba was phasing in an out of consciousness. He was not totally aware of what was happening around him but he knew that he was hurt and hurt badly. He was cold and could not feel his arms. His acute sense of hearing however allowed him to hear bits and pieces of the two emergency worker's conversations. The words that sent the message of the baby's demise stabbed his conscious core like a ragged dagger, tearing his insides. He heard them say the baby is dead. He screamed but no audible sounds came out and his screams faded in a deep chasm as he slid into darkness. The trauma of failure to keep the baby safe was overwhelming and Themba mentally beat himself into unconsciousness.

The assistant returned with two body bags and proceeded to remove the baby from Themba's tight clutches. Even in unconsciousness, Themba guarded the baby with his life. The assistant had to force the baby out of Themba's grip and as he did the baby squirmed with the rough handling. Startled the assistant almost dropped the baby as he was not expecting it to move. He tore the baby away from Themba's grip and brought it close to him. He could clearly see that the baby was alive and not injured. He took a closer look at Themba and although his breathing was shallow he saw his chest rise slightly as he breathed in and out. He called out to his partner,

"The baby is alive and not hurt and the Black man is also alive but barely. It looks like he was shot and bled all over the baby's blanket". The leader came over and peered at Themba and the baby and then as if shot from a catapult he sprung into action.

"Quickly bring that stretcher over and let's load the Black man into it. We need to get him to the emergency room". As the assistant looked for a place to lay the baby down, two more Indian emergency crew members joined them. The first crew member finding the timing to be perfect handed the baby to the arriving crew and said'

"This baby is alive and unhurt but will need medical attention. Take the baby to St Mary's Hospital immediately while we load up this Black man who is also alive but is in serious condition. We need to take him to the Provincial Hospital in Harding. He needs surgery quickly."

The arriving two brought a blanket from their ambulance and wrapped the baby in it. One of them climbed into the rear of the vehicle and cradled the baby in his arms whilst the other got into the driver's seat and drove off at high speed to St Mary's Hospital. The first two loaded Themba into the rear of their ambulance and proceeded to stabilize him by starting a drip and checking his vital signs. When they had done the bare minimum to stabilize Themba, they started up the vehicle, turned on the sirens and emergency lights and tore down the road to a nearby larger Provincial hospital where they knew that he would be adequately attended to. Neither of them gave any thought to the dead corpse of Johan they left behind, lying in the battle field. There would be hell to pay for them when this was over.

The nurse who met the ambulance at St Mary's Hospital took the baby from the emergency crew and rushed into the emergency room. The baby was now awake and started to cry a little. The nurse unwrapped the baby from the blanket and together with Rupin, who was now on duty proceeded to examine her. She was then promptly fed and burped. The nurse then proceeded to document her in the system so that in the morning they could attempt to find the parents. As she entered the details of the baby she came across a field for race. Without any hesitation she entered "Indian" into that field. The mandated apartheid system that governed one's destiny in South Africa just separated Buhle from her baby. The apartheid system in South Africa ensured that each race was allowed to develop separately with no mixing. The separate development however was not equitable. The baby looked very much like an Indian child and the nurse with one stroke of a pen changed the quality and destiny of this child's life for the future.

The next day the children social services staff would make an attempt to find the baby's mother. Since the comments added to the hospital's admittance record were that the child was found abandoned in a sugar cane field, the overly worked children social services worker would not bother to seek the mother. It was easier to send the child to the orphanage. Rupin watched the nurses fuss over the baby as she was so fragile but yet so adorable. Something inside him fluttered when his eyes met the baby's eyes. The baby's eye captivated him and he found himself having to look away to gain his composure.

Themba was rushed to the local Provincial Hospital and went straight into surgery to treat the gun shot wound. The South African Police were sent to stand guard on this political prisoner who was shot in the act of creating an uprising against the Government. This was an act of treason punishable by death. Since a white policeman was killed in action trying to maintain peace the South African Police commander sent word to the doctors to do every thing in their power to keep the prisoner alive so that they could execute him for crimes against the State.

CHAPTER 23

Mapoza literally dove through the door to Buhle's hut. He was out of breath and was sweating profusely. He looked around the hut for a hiding place and spotted Buhle on her bed. He looked at her and found that she looked pale but peaceful as she lay there. He wondered whether she was alive as he expected her to jump up startled when he made such a dramatic entrance. He decided that right now he did not have time to find out, he had to save himself. The days events came rushing back to him including the plans for the baby in a few hours. To him all of this seemed to have happened a long time ago. Mapoza heard the dogs barking and sheer terror consumed him. All he could think about is that they brought more dogs.

The riot squad led by the frenzied dogs advanced upon the village. In true battle formation they surrounded the village. This general area around the village was the home of the Inkatha Freedom Party, called the IFP. These were turbulent times for the Zulu nation as they fought for liberation from the oppressive White rule. The Inkatha Freedom Party believed strongly that peaceful options were needed to bring about change in the country. Some White extremists tended to instigate raids into the villages and made it seem like Black on Black struggle. With this threat always looming over their heads the Zulu able bodied men were always on guard and prepared. When the riot squad moved into the village under cover of darkness the Zulu inhabitants prepared to defend themselves.

As the Zulus fighter's emerged from dark hiding spots the riot squad recoiled and went into battle mode. Under the tense atmosphere a couple of the young immature armed riot squad members opened fire into huts and in no time at all there was total massacre. Mapoza realized that he did not stand a chance alone in this hut when they did a hut by hut search. He left the hut under the cover of the mayhem. He did not get very far as one of the riot squad troops slammed him with his baton knocking Mapoza to the ground. He was handcuffed and thrown into the back of one of the police vans. The Sangoma seeing her son being attacked emerged from her hiding position and ran after her son. A young nervous riot squad guard saw this dark figure with a ghostly white face and long hair flying open in the wind rushing towards him, screeching. He panicked and brought down the Sangoma with the burst of his automatic rifle.

It was all over quickly. The silence that followed after the last shot was fired covered the village like a dark shroud. One guard whispered anxiously to his team member,

"What just happened here?"

Commander Villiers looked around at the dead bodies and a cold sweat poured down his face. He thought to himself that this was not justified. He needed to reassure his troops in thinking that they were provoked and had to defend themselves. He did not want any second guessing as to what should have happened. He barked out orders in Afrikaans,

"Take care of any causalities on our side. Carefully search each of the huts for anymore threats and subdue them. Collect all the weapons and photograph them as evidence." He turned to his assistant and ordered,

"Transport the dead to the government mortuary for processing." The assistant gathered a small group from the squad and started to collect the bodies. Each of the bodies were carried by two guards and thrown like a bag of sand onto the back of a flat bed truck. Two guards entered Buhle's hut and saw here lying there and one of them grabbed her by the ankles while the other grabbed her by her arms and half carried and half dragged her to the truck. After collecting several dead bodies they did not take any time to check if the victims were dead or alive. Buhle was thrown on top of some dead bodies and there she lay unconscious among the dead. The assistant documented the number of bodies and instructed the driver to transport the bodies to the government mortuary. The few injured Zulus were loaded into a truck and transported to the nearby Provincial Hospital.

The attendants at the government mortuary were alerted that a number of bodies are being delivered and they scrambled to make space in this already crowded mortuary. The truck arrived and backed into the loading dock for easy off-loading of the bodies. The attendants brought out several stainless carts for easy off loading and proceeded to off—load the bodies. The attendant that removed Buhle from the truck was struck with how differently her body handled compared to the others. Her clothes were blood soaked, some blood stains from her and others from her contact with the dead bodies on the truck. When he carried her she was limp and supple, unlike the dead weight of the other victims. He put her on one the stainless steel cart and set her aside. He then helped to complete the off loading of the other bodies.

When the truck left, the attendant, curious about the one body decided to examine her further. It did not take him long to establish that this person was alive, just barely alive. The attendant alerted his supervisor and an ambulance was summoned from the hospital to transport Buhle. On arrival at the Provincial Hospital Buhle was admitted and the doctors stabilized her condition. She was critically ill from the loss of blood and was immediately given blood transfusion. Attempts to wake Buhle were unsuccessful and the doctors had concluded that the patient had slipped into a coma. They concluded that the comatose condition was brought about after a recent difficult birth that resulted in excessive bleeding. This trauma at birth was not addressed in a timely manner and was the reason for her condition.

Attacks on Black villages in the Homelands were so common that it was barely a news item. The attacks were perpetrated by rival faction groups, as well as, by extremist White groups looking to disrupt and create chaos in an already turbulent political climate. The report in the local news paper the next day appeared in the middle of the paper in a small column. The reporter stated that several Blacks were killed when they clashed with the riot squad during a freedom rally that got out of control.

What the reporter did not know was that all of this tragedy was born in a moment of indiscretion in a sugar cane field nine months ago.

CHAPTER 24

One reporter by the name of James Anderson tagged the massacre on the Zulu village in his weekend editorial of the South Coast Times as the "Harding Massacre". He was the only reporter that attempted to raise public outcry for what he considered to be unjustified killings by the police. The article that was well researched by James talked about a mute being shot in the sugar cane field and in recounting the carnage also mentioned that emergency crew members found one woman in a coma and had taken her to the local hospital. At least twenty or more men, women and children were killed; the article reported. The article was buried in a supplemental page in the English Sunday paper and failed to raise public concern. Those that saw the editorial heading "The Harding Massacre" happened to turn to this supplement looking for supermarket specials and promptly scanned the paper for bargains. Most of the White South Africans were tired of reading about Steve Biko who died in captivity and turned a blind eye to more Black killings. Steve Biko was the leader of the Black Consciousness Movement and was arrested under the Terrorism Act No 83 of 1967. The massacre at Harding being in the shadows of Steve Biko's death, instead of making history went into oblivion.

Rupin went home after spending the night of the Harding massacre at the hospital. He decided to resume his normal routine in life and not confront Sheila with what transpired the night he watched them. He would add that event to his arsenal of transgressions committed by his wife and friend and bring it out when the time was right. At this time Rupin was preoccupied with the Harding massacre and the baby at the hospital. The image of that baby had derailed his charge for vengeance and he needed some time to think. Sheila was moody and distant and Rupin found that strange. He would have expected her to be happy as she had just spent an evening with Devraj when she thought that he was away. Rupin did notice that Sheila had returned to her normal selfish person, and was no longer affectionate and seductive.

Rupin had neglected to treat his Klinefelter's syndrome and his condition was worsening. Rupin's intense obsession to control his wife and friend combined with his psychosocial morbidity transformed him into a cunning and dangerous predator. This obsession was consuming him so much that he had neglected his own health problems.

Rupin could not shake the image of the child at the hospital, especially her eyes. Those eyes bore into his soul and he had an uncanny feeling that he was looking at someone he knew. That Sunday, Rupin was reading the weekend newspaper and came across the "Harding Massacre" editorial and being curious he read the whole article. The cogs wheels in his head started to turn and he reflected on the events of the Harding massacre. He was still in his pensive mood when a tap on his shoulder brought him back to reality. A voice said,

"Hi, I will give a penny for your thoughts". Rupin looked up and there stood Devraj, with a broad smile on his face. Rupin looked at Devraj and nodded. Like a photographic flashbulb that leaves an image at the back of your eye, Rupin could see the baby's eyes superimposed over Devraj's eyes. Rupin looked deeply at Devraj's eyes and suddenly it gelled in his mind. It all made sense; he knew now what drew him to that baby girl. He knew who the father was. Rupin turned to Devraj and said with a cunning smile on his face,

"It will cost you more than a penny" and thought to himself, "the seed that you planted has come to expose you." Getting out of his lounge chair, Rupin invited Devraj to sit and make himself comfortable and then proceed to make some excuse to head back to the hospital. As he gathered his work bag he thought to himself that it will definitely cost Devraj more than just a penny, a lot more. Smiling at Devraj, Rupin said,

"I have an emergency at the hospital and have to leave. Stay here and keep Sheila company, I will be back in an hour or so". Devraj feigned disappointment at being left alone, but he needed to talk to Sheila and this was the perfect opportunity. Devraj tapped Rupin on his shoulders and said,

"Oh Rupin there is no rest for the wicked" and chuckled at his own sense of humor. Rupin smiled and left Devraj alone with Sheila, but he did not care. He had a new weapon to defeat both Sheila and Devraj together. Rupin drove back to the hospital and headed for the nursery. Looking at the baby he now saw the resemblance. He was convinced that

Devraj was the father of this baby girl. The birth of this child exhumed the tragedy that was buried so deeply in the souls of three people.

The next day Rupin called the children services and made a formal request to adopt the baby. Rupin saw this baby as a trump card to hold over Devraj and a leverage to use with Sheila. Rupin was not planning to let Devraj know his theory about the relationship of this baby as in his diabolical mind he wanted to watch how this would play out with him manipulating the outcome. The children services representative was extremely pleased to know that Rupin was planning to adopt this baby. The alternative for the baby was to be placed in an already crowded orphanage. There were no formal review and approvals to be sought and so with a nod from children services a child crossed racial lines in an apartheid society designed to keep them apart.

The baby was beautiful. Her stunning eyes captivated everyone who looked at her. Rupin had Sheila accompany him to the hospital the next day and in the confines of Rupin's office, a pawn was placed on this tragic chess board for the entertainment of the king and queen. Rupin had no doubt that Sheila would love this baby and there would be no place for Devraj in her life. The tragic irony in the situation as Rupin contemplated was that Devraj was going to lose Sheila because of his own flesh and blood. Rupin also speculated that Devraj would be drawn to this baby instinctively and so he would want to maintain his relationship with Sheila and the baby. Rupin however held the strings to these marionettes for he knew that Sheila would detest Devraj if she knew what he had done. Of course Rupin would inject only so much of information into Devraj to keep just enough doubt to ruin him slowly. Rupin was pleased with himself, he was in control.

The first time that Sheila laid her eyes on the baby girl, her heart melted. The baby was beautiful with striking eyes. The eyes reminded her of someone but she could not figure out who that was. She picked up the baby and hugged her. Sheila was so enthralled with this baby and knowing that Rupin had arranged all of this for her, she felt guilty for having treated him so poorly. She went over to Rupin and kissed him gently and quietly whispered in his ears, "thank you". She then made a promise to her self that she was going to make her marriage work. She was going to change the way she treated Rupin; she decided to be good to him and make up for all those times that she had mistreated him. If only she knew the tangled web she was trapped in and how all of this would play out.

That day, with very little ceremony or formalities, the little baby girl went with Rupin and Sheila to her new home. Devraj had heard that Rupin and Sheila were adopting a baby and he was excited and really happy for them. He anxiously waited for the afternoon to visit Rupin and Sheila so that he could welcome the baby and congratulate the proud parents. If only he knew that he also was entangled in a web with no way out.

That afternoon Devraj stopped at the house with a little gift bag for the baby. He stopped by the local clothing store for babies and bought a pretty pink baby's blanket with matching towels. Devraj was excited with the new arrival as he expected that it would fill the void in Sheila's life and she would not be looking for love outside her marriage. He talked to her when Rupin had left and cleared the air. They agreed to forget that incident and never mention it again.

When Devraj arrived at Rupin's home Sheila was sitting on the porch gently rocking the baby humming to her self. Devraj watched her as he approached and was pleased to see how much Sheila had changed. She looked radiant and the image of her holding the baby was precious. Rupin was standing idly around waiting to see Devraj's reaction when he saw the baby. Devraj approached Sheila and the baby and as he came closer Sheila peeled away the blanket to show Devraj the baby's face. With love and pride Shelia looked down at the baby and with a barely audible voice she said'

"This is Nina; we named her Nina because she has beautiful eyes". Devraj knew that in the Indian language Nina meant "beautiful eyes".

As Devraj looked at the baby's eyes he felt a sudden quickening in his heart rate and for a brief instance he felt naked and exposed, as if someone opened his soul wide and spilled out its contents for the world to see. He quickly regained his composure and asked if he could carry Nina for a moment.

The transition in Devraj was very brief but Rupin did not miss it. He was watching Devraj's face intently and saw his eyes cloud over. Rupin smiled; for the first time everything was going his way.

CHAPTER 25

André Pretorius spent a quiet weekend at home. He found that these days he spent a lot of time alone at home with his dog. He often thought of Themba and wondered where he was and how he was doing. André went to his cabin often, hoping that he would see Themba again but always came home disappointed. Even his dog, Misty would scan the horizon and sniff the air expectantly hoping that Themba would turn up.

André flipped through the weekend papers and as always he turned to the obituaries section. For some odd reason André was drawn to this section as it allowed him to read the sentiments expressed by family members and friends of the departed. Having lost his wife tragically he found comfort from reading about the loss of others as it made him feel part of a larger population with the same misfortune to lose a loved one instead of feeling that he was singled out.

As he read the obituaries he came across the one written for Johan Botha. André read about the heroic accounts of Johan and how he died fighting to crush an uprising in a nearby sugar cane field. André was bothered about the reports of the violence as he knew from his experiences that the Zulu people were advocates of peaceful negotiation for liberation from this oppressive Government. The death of Steve Biko while he was in police custody had sickened André and the increasing tension in the country was really concerning him. André put the paper aside and picked up his Bible and retreated to his bedroom. He had found great comfort in reading the Bible whenever he felt this low in his life.

André could not sleep that night, he tossed and turned and finally gave up trying to sleep. He got up and turned on the light. He was expecting to see Misty asleep at the side of the bed but he was surprised to see the dog sitting on his blanket watching him. He reached over and stroked the dog and said,

"I see that you cannot sleep as well. Let's go get something to drink". And with his tail wagging, Misty followed André into the kitchen. André poured himself a glass of milk and gave a dog biscuit to Misty. Returning to his lounge, he grabbed the news paper and started reading the page where the paper was left the night before. His eyes fell on Johan's heroic attempt at crushing the Black uprising and as he continued reading he came across the statement that said that Johan was killed by a mute Zulu man. André almost dropped the paper; what were the chances that they were referring to Themba. With his heart rate quickening at that thought, André read on. The article in the paper reported that the police had the mute Black person in custody and that he would be tried for treason and sentenced to death.

André's mind raced in all different directions. As sure as he was that Themba could not be involved he could not help but worry that it might have been Themba caught up in some misunderstanding. André knew how easily a mute could be misunderstood.

The next morning, André drove to the Harding police station to inquire about the article he read in the paper. The police station was a hostile place with dogs barking incessantly and police vehicles coming and going like bees to a hive. André went up to the front desk and waited to be attended to. After a while a policeman came up the desk and asked André what he had wanted. André showed the policeman the article in the paper and asked,

"Where is the Black man that was arrested for the shooting?" The policeman was taken aback with this inquiry. It was not common for someone to come looking for Black inmates. With a bemused look on his face he asked,

"Why do you want to know?" André was quick to realize that he may be stepping into a lot of trouble here and so he was careful with his response.

"I wanted to see if it was the same man who tried to rob me the other day, he too was mute". André felt sick to his stomach as he lied about his true intentions, especially since in his mind he was thinking of Themba. The policeman smiled broadly and with a thick Afrikaner accent he said,

"It probably was. These kaffirs are too lazy to work; they would rather steal". André's stomach twisted at that stereotypical remark and he wanted to reach over and grab the policeman by the throat. André felt ashamed for having started this line of conversion and silently begged

Themba for forgiveness. The policeman, obviously very familiar with this shooting said,

"He is at the Natal Provincial Hospital under police guard. He was shot but the Doctors saved his life so that he could be hanged until he is dead". Seeing the ironical humor in what he had just said he burst out laughing banging the counter top with the palms of his hands as he did so. André took this opportunity to turn on his heels and leave the police station. When he got outside to his car he felt the cool breeze on his face and he felt better. He needed to get out in the open and get some fresh air. He had lived in this apartheid society for so long that he had become desensitized to its inhumanity. André could not believe how much resentment the White policeman had for the Black people and they probably never knew them. André found himself apologizing to Themba for the unkind and humiliating remarks made by the policeman.

André did not waste anymore time. He raced to the Provincial hospital in Harding, all the while praying that it was not Themba. And if it was then he hoped that his injuries were not serious and that there was a simple explanation to this misunderstanding. Arriving at the hospital, André did not bother to find parking for his car. He left his car in the emergency parking and rushed into the hospital reception lobby. The hospital was a typical government hospital with almond colored tiled walls and grey heavy duty linoleum floors. Entering the building, André was expecting to see a reception desk with an attendant but he was surprised to see an open area with wooden benches lined in rows. The benches were filled with Black men and women and in some cases there were children of all ages from newly born to teenagers. Waiting amongst these folks were a number of Indian people also with small children. André was surprised to see that quite of few of the people waiting to be seen had packed food for their long wait. A lot of them had small food containers and a container for drinks. André was saddened that these folks needed to actually pack a lunch for a trip to the doctor. He was used to calling a doctor for an appointment and he was ashamed that he had become frustrated when he had to wait an hour after his appointment time.

Some of them looked up at him expectantly, hoping that he was a doctor come to help the understaffed and overworked nurses and doctors at this hospital. These people arrived at six in the morning with the hope that they will be seen by lunch time. If they were not seen by four in the afternoon then they would have to come back the next morning.

André scanned the room hoping to find an employee of the hospital that could help him. An Indian nurse came out of a closed room with a clipboard in her hand and was scanning the area looking for someone. André quickly rushed to her and asked,

"I am looking for a patient who was brought in a few days ago. Where would I go to find what ward he is located in?" Annoyed that he was pestering her and without bothering to pick her head from her clipboard she said in a curt tone,

"You have to go to General Admittance" and with that response she opened a door to a closed room and disappeared. André was dumb founded; where was General Admittance? He pitied the desperate Black patient who could not speak English trying to get directions. It seemed to André that the nurse was probably overworked and underpaid and was frustrated with the working conditions at this hospital. He tried not to be angry at the nurse as she was only a reflection of her environment. André looked around at the signs hanging in the corridors and walked around the corridors hoping to see some signage that would lead him to General Admittance.

The hospital was a maze of corridors and André was beginning to think that he would not be able to find his way out when he saw a sign over a desk that read "General Admittance". His heart leaped in anticipation as he approached the busy desk. There was a line of people waiting to be attended to. A young Black girl was busy entering data into a huge computer terminal as she asked for information in Zulu, from the person in front of her. As she was the only one there, André stepped up to the counter and said,

"Miss, can you help me, I am looking for a patient at this hospital?" Without breaking stride at her typing, she said rather firmly'

"Wait your turn. Go to the end of the line and wait until it is your turn". With that she continued to type at her terminal. André persisted,

"If you could spare on moment...", he was cut short when the girl stopped typing, rage filled her face as she looked up ready to explode at this intruder. She opened her mouth and started to say,

"I said!" And then seeing a White man in front of her, she quickly backed down and said obediently,

"What can I do for you". André looked over his shoulders to see if some important person had just stepped up behind him. Realizing that she was talking to him, he said,

"I am looking for the mute person who was shot at the recent massacre in Harding. The police told me that he was brought here for medical attention". The attendant knew who André was referring to as she was in duty that night when the mute was brought in. She remembered that there was a lot of activity that night especially since he was being guarded by heavily armed policemen.

Without needing to look up the ward he was in, she said,

"Take the elevator to the fourth floor. He is in the men's ward in section K". André did not want to push his luck and ask for more directions at this time so he said apologetically,

"Thank you and I am sorry for interrupting you" and turned on his heels and looked for signs that would point him to the elevator.

André was pleased that he found the bank of elevators without too much of an effort and pressed the button for going up. When the elevator arrived at the ground floor André stepped into the elevator and had to stand sideways because there was a gurney with a body completely covered also in the elevator. The orderly that accompanied the gurney was reading a magazine and did not seem to be in a hurry to get to any particular floor. The blood stained sheet showed the outline of a large man and André wondered what tragedy had taken his life. André wondered why the body on the gurney was going up when the mortuary was in the basement floor. André looked at the orderly who was unconcerned with which direction the elevator was headed and he realized that he was obviously using this time to take a break. André was relieved when the elevator arrived at the fourth floor. He quickly stepped out of the elevator and exhaled as he was unconsciously holding his breath in the elevator.

Luck was on his side as Section K was directly on his right and he turned in that direction. He found the male ward opposite the female ward and spotted the two armed guards chatting and laughing at some private joke. They looked up when André came towards the male ward and when they saw a White man, they continued with their conversation and never gave him another glance. André walked into the ward and he saw rows of beds with Black patients lying under light grey hospital sheets. Some of the patients were gravely ill with intravenous drips while others just lay there. Those that were conscious turned and looked at the new arrival as it was new entertainment for their boredom.

André walked slowly past each bed looking carefully at each patient. Many eyes followed him as he walked down one side and started up the other side. André was anxious for what he might find and the atmosphere here was eerie. He heard the occasional moan peppered with a raspy cough coming from the patients and the smell of disinfectant burned his nostrils. On his way back past the beds he spotted handcuffs and a Black man's hand tethered to the bed rails. He stood at the end of the bed afraid to look at the patient. His eyes slowly traveled from the handcuffs up the man's arm to his chest that was heavily bandaged and he knew that this was his man. But was it his man, his Themba? André raised his eyes and focused on the face. He had to grab the bed rails for support as his legs buckled. His heart sank as he looked upon Themba's face which was badly bruised. His lip was cut and one eye was swollen shut. His face was puffy and it was obvious that he was beaten as well as being shot. André regained his composure and started to go up to Themba who was sleeping soundly, obviously heavily drugged when he heard some one say,

"Hey you, get away from that man". André turned to see one of the guards come towards him, arms raised in a halt pose.

"That man is under police guard and you cannot go near him. What is your business with him any way?" André had to think quickly,

"I thought I recognized him. I am looking for my gardener who was admitted to this hospital yesterday but it is not him". André walked away from the bed pretending to look at the remaining beds. The guard's eyes followed him suspiciously and now more pairs of eyes watched him from the hospital beds with renewed curiosity.

As André made a hasty exit from the ward, one of the guards picked up his radio and retreated to a quiet corner of the corridor. He turned his back and speaking in hushed tones, he relayed the account of André's visit to a guard on the hospital grounds.

CHAPTER 26

D r Nirmal Ansari was a tall man of Indian descent. He wore thick black rimmed glasses with high powered corrective lenses that made his eyes look larger than they actually were. He had a serious nature about him and rarely smiled, but when he did, his smile was captivating and infectious. He had a reputation of being impatient with the nurses and demanded perfection. So it was not surprising that when the nurses saw that he was on duty this Monday morning, they assigned the new nurse Lungile to his rounds for the day. Nurse Lungile had no clue who Dr Ansari was and had no inclination of his reputation. She was excited to make her first ward round with the doctor. She gathered her notebook and went to the doctor's lounge to see if Dr Ansari was ready to make his rounds through the women's ward in Section K of the Natal Provincial Hospital.

Dr Ansari being tall tended to take long strides and Nurse Lungile had a tough time keeping up with him as he made his way through the long corridors. She tried to break the ice with him with some small talk but it fell on deaf ears. She resigned herself to just taking instructions. When they got to the women's ward in Section K, Dr Ansari asked to examine the most critical patients first. He did this so that if he ran out of time he would have at least attended to the ones that needed his attention the most. Dr Ansari was noted for his logical approach to medicine Nurse Lungile was not prepared for this triage method and looked at the doctor blankly. He glared at her through his thick glasses and Nurse Lungile could see his eyes bulge with anger, the thick lenses exaggerating the image. Dr Ansari looked at her for the first time and said,

"I haven't seen your face before, are you new here?" Nurse Lungile nodded her head in embarrassment as if being new was a bad thing. Dr Ansari's face softened and smiling his captivating smile he said,

"So they assigned you to me on your first day; that was cruel of them. OK, follow me and take notes of the order we follow. Tomorrow you will lead the way". Showing his caring and mentoring side, Dr Nirmal Ansari smiled again and led Nurse Lungile down the ward. A new friendship was forged. Nurse Lungile was relieved and happily followed him. As they went from one patient to another Nurse Lungile was impressed with the doctor's command of the Zulu language. He would speak to each Zulu patient in Zulu and would say things like "Unjani?" when he asked how are you, or when he wanted the patient to breathe in and out he would say "Donsa umoya and Khipha umoya." She was also impressed with his bedside manners and when he was leaving the patient he would usually say "Sala kahle". The phrase translated to English meant "Stay well" but was commonly used as a parting greeting for goodbye.

Nurse Lungile was feeling good about these rounds until they came to the bed with an unconscious young Black woman lying on it. Dr Ansari asked,

"Where did this woman come from?" As he asked the question, he looked through her chart at her bedside. In the space for patient's name, the words "Unknown Zulu woman" were written and no other identification was given. The chart indicated that this patient was in a coma most likely from excessive bleeding during child birth and a subsequent condition known as Amniotic Fluid Embolism.

Dr Ansari asked, "Where did she come from? What about her next of kin?" Nurse Lungile gave him a blank look and shrugged her shoulders. Dr Ansari was frustrated that so little was known about this woman. It bothered him that a person can show up in hospital and nobody cares to find her.

Dr Ansari asked, "Where is the baby that she had given birth to?" Nurse Lungile still did not have any answers. Dr Ansari sadly continued,

"Well I guess nobody cares about the baby too. We have done everything we can do; there is nothing more we can do with her. We stopped the bleeding and it is now up to her to snap out of it".

Dr Ansari used his forefinger to push his glasses up on his nose and looked at Buhle lying in a coma on the bed. With a hint of sadness in his voice he said,

"She is beautiful and so young to have this happen to her". Leaving her bed for the next bed on his rounds, Dr Ansari said,

"If she does not come out of her coma in a week then have her transferred to King Edward Hospital in Durban. They may be able to help her". Nurse Lungile furiously made some notes in her note book and then followed Dr Ansari to the next patient.

Across the corridor, Themba groaned as he slowly recovered consciousness. He hurt all over and his mind was a turbulent storm of fleeting thoughts. The one thought that exploded in his mind and jolted him into reality was the baby he held so tightly before he passed out. He opened the eye that was not swollen shut and looked around him. His eye darted back and forth across the beds in the ward and as he tried to get up he realized that both his hands were handcuffed to the bed rails. Themba was a free spirited soul and the only restrictions he had were ones that were self imposed. Themba had never been forcibly restrained in the past and this situation brought terror and rage to him. Ignoring the pain brought on by his movement he bucked his body on the bed like a bull in a rodeo and tugged at the handcuffs. His squeals of terror reverberated across the ward scaring the other patients. The other patients were terrified of this madman who sounded like a wounded animal and those that could get out of their beds scrambled for the exits. In an instant there was complete pandemonium. The guards alerted by the chaos ran into the room to control the situation. One guard radioed to his colleague on the hospital grounds for back up. The guard on the hospital grounds had just finished writing down the license plate on André's car as André drove off when he received the call. He put his note book away and ran into the hospital with his radio to his mouth, calling in for more backup.

Dr Ansari and Lungile looked at each other when they heard the commotion. They went to the corridor to see what was happening and saw the guard calling for help. Dr Ansari asked,

"What is happening?" The guard stuck his hand out and ordered,

"Get out of here. That madman who killed Johan and badly injured so many others in our squad is on the rampage. I have called for backup, so get out of the way". With that said he un-holstered his gun and ran into the Male ward of Section K.

Dr Ansari and Nurse Lungile, fearing for their lives, took off running and headed for the stairwell. They were not taking any chances waiting for the elevator.

CHAPTER 27

As the second guard rushed into the ward he saw his colleague standing and watching Themba buck against the restraints. Although he had his baton drawn he was too afraid to approach the bed. Themba was a muscular man and as he lay there with the sheets torn away from him from the struggle to free him self, he looked like a formidable adversary. Themba's muscles rippled throughout his naked body as he strained against the handcuffs and his eyes burned with terror and rage. The deep throated sound that came from him no longer sounded like a squealing pig, he sounded more like a large enraged lion. The guard raised his baton in a show of strength but he was too far away to strike Themba. Trying to make an impact he struck the bed rail which such force that it resonated all the way down the corridor and echoed in the stairwell. That show of strength only served to enrage Themba even more and he snarled at the guard, his white teeth gnashing at the empty air. The guard took a few steps back in retreat. Most patients that were able to move from their beds had either crawled or run from the ward. Others that were conscious and could not leave their beds just pulled the sheet over their heads and pretended that they were invisible. The sounds of Themba roaring like a lion carried into the women's ward across the corridor and deep down in Buhle's core it touched her soul. Nobody was there to see the look on her face as she responded with love and pride when she heard Themba. Her Themba was back and he was going to stand up for himself. The sound of Themba's voice lit a flame in the darkness that was slowly consuming her and it fluttered against the storm of dread that was pulling her into the abyss.

The second guard rushed in and took in the chaotic scene. He raised his gun and approaching Themba's bedside. He pointed it at Themba's head hoping to scare him into submission. Themba snarled at the guard like a caged lion and the guard involuntarily stepped back. Themba jerked at the handcuff and the bed rocked on his castors moving it away from the wall. Blood seeped into the bandages that covered the gunshot wound as the stitches gave way in his chest. Themba bucked again and jerked at the handcuffs and with a sound like nails on a chalk board the bed rail gave way and clanked on to the floor. The handcuff on Themba's right hand came free from the bedrails and Themba lurched up in his bed emitting a blood curdling scream at the guard. The guard reacted instinctively as he raised the gun and brought the butt of his heavy service revolver hard against the side of Themba's head. The sound of the thud that came from the blow was followed by an ominous silence as Themba slumped back onto the bed. Sounds of the whirling ceiling fans and the ticking wall clock in the ward seemed to slowly dominate the ward. Frightened heads peered cautiously from covered bed sheets. In the women's ward across the corridor a flame in a troubled soul took fire and illuminated the world of Buhle.

******

André sat in his lounge chair and sipped on a hot cup of tea. Ever since he got back from the hospital he had been preoccupied, working through what he needed to do. It was obvious that Themba needed help and he felt compelled to help. Deep in the pit of his stomach André was really concerned for Themba's life. He remembered all too clearly the accounts of Steve Biko and his tragic death whilst in police custody. Since 1966, the General Laws Amendment Act allowed the police to detain "suspected terrorists" for fourteen days for interrogation purposes. This fourteen day period was increased to ninety days, then to one hundred and eighty days and finally to an indefinite period. It was common knowledge that the police used this detention period to torture a suspected terrorist and extract false confessions.

André shuddered when he thought about Themba's quiet nature and his inability to express himself audibly in an interrogation. His instinct told him that Themba was innocent of the charge of murder and all this was a huge misunderstanding, but how does one go about defending him. Given the circumstances, André knew that if he didn't help, Themba was a dead man. Either he would he tortured and killed during his detention or he would be hanged after being found guilty by the South African judicial system.

That was the other problem. Trial by jury was abolished in nineteen sixty nine. Themba would be tried as a security case by a special superior court and sentenced to death by a Judge who was appointed by the State President. He would not be represented adequately and he had no notoriety that would offer him some protection by the international community. And since there were no Non-white judges at this time Themba would face the wrath of a White judge who would see Themba as a terrorist and a threat to the judge's own existence.

This did not look good. André racked his mind for a contact at the former SADAF, the South African Defense and Aid Fund. This organization which was formed in 1960 and primarily helped in political cases but was banned by the Government in nineteen sixty six. André felt that this organization would be a good place to contact an attorney who might take on Themba's case.

André was mulling over these thoughts in his head as he looked out of his window. His attention was momentarily drawn to a white Ford Cortina that was slowly cruising down the road. The car slowed down at the front of André house and paused momentarily and then sped off. The car looked like a Government issue vehicle for it sported three long antennas and had a number stenciled in black on the trunk cover. André thought that it was strange for he lived in a quiet cul-de-sac and it was rare to find strangers drive down the road. André dismissed the concern as he had more important issues on his mind.

The next morning André got up at the break of dawn. He had a restless night and was concerned about Themba. André retrieved the drawings that Themba had given him during the time they spent together at his cabin and those drawings brought back fond memories of their time together. They had used those drawings as a communication vehicle until Themba had learnt to use sign language. André had paused on Themba's drawing of Buhle and he remembered how beautiful she was. Themba obviously loved Buhle deeply as the drawing tended to reflect his passion. Themba had relayed through sign language his love for Buhle and André felt that he had known her for a long time. André had remembered how it amazed him to watch how quickly Themba learnt new things.

He decided to make another visit to the hospital to check on Themba and he hoped that the guards would have changed shifts and he would not have to explain himself to the guards from the day before. He decided that if he is questioned about his visit then he will state that he was there to see Themba and let them know that Themba is not alone. After all André felt that he was not breaking any laws by visiting a friend in hospital.

André drove to the hospital in the morning and he had a strange feeling that he was being followed. He had glanced in his rearview mirror a few times and he caught a glimpse of a white Ford Cortina a few car lengths away. André tried to not let that bother him as he had more important things to take care off. Arriving at the hospital André raced up to the ward on the fourth floor where he saw Themba the day before. André braced himself as he prepared to exit the elevator as he knew that the guards would be there. André became alarmed when he exited the elevator and did not see any guards.

André rushed into the ward and headed towards the bed that Themba had occupied the day before. André halted in his tracks as he approached the bed and his heart sank. The bed was empty and completely made up as if it was never occupied. André desperately looked around the ward, just in case Themba was moved but there were no signs of him. André screamed at the patients,

"Where is he? Where did they take him to? What happened to him?" All he got back were blank stares from the patients and they quickly looked away or closed their eyes feigning sleep. André ran out of the ward and collided with Dr Nirmal Ansari who was rushing to the female ward with Nurse Lungile. André apologized to Dr Ansari and grabbing his white lab coat lapels he asked desperately,

"Doctor, there was a patient in the male ward yesterday and today he is gone. Please tell me what had happened to him?" Dr Ansari shook André off and without looking at him quietly said,

"Be quiet don't say another word; you never know who is listening and will turn you in. Just follow me and listen".

CHAPTER 28

Dr Nirmal Ansari entered the Woman's ward with Nurse Lungile by his side and André trailing behind him. He quietly said without looking at André, when you leave the hospital on your way out glance at the emergency contact numbers and make a mental note of my home number. My name is Dr Nirmal Ansari and please don't be obvious as you make a note of my number. There may be people who are following you. Call me tonight after nine and I will tell you what I know.

Dr Ansari continued to walk to Buhle's bedside ignoring André as he did. André was momentarily confused and stood there trying to digest what he had just heard. Numbed with the prospect of the reality of being followed, André stood there and watched Dr Ansari talk to the young Zulu woman on the bed. As his eyes focused on the patient, he had a strange feeling that he knew her. André went closer to the bed and got a closer look at her but he could not place her face although he was almost sure that he knew the woman. Dr Ansari greeted the woman and asked her name,

"Sawubona, Ungubani igama lakho na?" The young Zulu woman weakly answered "

"Iyaphila, Buhle" saying that she was well and her name was Buhle. Barely audible she whispered some words but Dr Ansari did not understand what she said. André on the other hand was trained in listening skills and he was sure that he heard her ask for Themba and also used the word "Ingane". Although André was not totally fluent in the Zulu language he knew that "Ingane" was "baby" or "child" in Zulu. His heart raced as he finally made the connection. This was the girl that Themba had so passionately drawn to describe Buhle for André. Dr Ansari turned to Nurse Lungile and said,

"She is still weak but I expect that she will recover quickly. She is strong and young and with some nourishment she will recover completely. Let's check on her again in an hour or so". Dr Ansari then draped his stethoscope over his neck and shoulders and turning he left the ward. He completely ignored André as he passed him and made his way to the exit. Nurse Lungile followed him making notes in her little note pad.

André went to Buhle's bedside and grabbing a small metal stool by her bedside, he sat down and watched her sleep. About fifteen minutes later Buhle fluttered her eyelids and cautiously opened her eyes. She saw André sitting by her bedside and his warm eyes and pleasant smile comforted her. André said quietly,

"My name is André and I am a friend of Themba". Buhle remembered Themba trying to use signs and pictures to relay the name "André" to her and he had done a good job at getting that name across to her. Buhle's smile broadened and some color came to her face. She said a little more energetically,

"I know who you are, thank you for coming. Please tell me where Themba and the baby are, please , please I want to see them" This was so difficult for André as the he did not read any mention of any newly born babies being found at the site. He presumed that the baby was also killed in the massacre and all the bodies were buried at a mass grave. André looked at Buhle and said '

"Themba is OK but was shot by the police, I saw him yesterday." Buhle tensed her body anticipating the worst. André continued quickly,

"They must have transferred him to another hospital and I promise that I will find out where. I will also look for the baby. You must rest now and I will come back and give you more information".

As André turned to leave, Buhle reached out and held his wrist hoping to stop him from leaving. André's presence had comforted her and she did not want him to go. Her grip was weak and her hands slipped off his wrists as he moved away. André turned, his eyes now moist with tears, and looked at Buhle. With as much confidence as he could muster he said

"I will find Themba and ask him where the baby is. Please don't worry, get some rest". Without waiting for a response André hurried out of the ward. Buhle watched with renewed hope that André will find Themba and bring him and the baby to her.

When André left the ward and turned the corner he wiped a tear from his eyes with the back of his palm. He knew that with the massacre as was reported, the baby did not stand a chance. He did not have the heart to tell Buhle what he suspected so he decided that when he found out beyond all doubt what had happened then he would tell her the truth. As André passed the nurses station he saw the emergency numbers board, André glanced at the numbers on the board and nonchalantly scanned the numbers. When he came across Dr Nirmal Ansari's number he memorized it and proceeded to the elevator to exit the floor.

André was preoccupied as he left the hospital parking and proceeded down to the onramp that led him to the highway to his home. André had heard many horror stories about police interrogation and torture and usually focused on other matters as it was unsettling and did not directly affect his life, until now. Now he was faced with the reality of this cruelty and he, for the first time, was scared. He didn't know who he could turn to for help. As he changed from the fast lane to the slower lane to prepare his exit off the highway, he glanced at his review mirror to see if it was safe to do so. His heart skipped a beat when he saw the white Ford Cortina in his review mirror also changing lanes with him.

André tried not to panic. He knew he could not get away from that Ford as his fairly new Toyota Corolla was not as fast as those specially modified police cars. André used his turn signals and took the next off ramp, exiting the highway. He nervously looked at his review mirror and a cold feeling off dread swept over him when he saw the Ford Cortina do the same. He thought to himself, "Why am I panicking? I didn't do anything wrong. I haven't broken any laws." But no matter how hard he tried to convince himself that he was safe, his gut feeling told him to run.

André decided that he would just drive home and not look again in the rearview mirror. He would watch his speed carefully and not give this policeman following him any reason to stop him. If only he could get away from this deserted road and arrive at his neighborhood he would feel safer. He knew that there was always someone in the cul-de-sac and that thought gave him some comfort.

The inside of his car was suddenly illuminated by a flashing blue light. André groaned as he looked in his rearview mirror and saw the white Ford Cortina behind him with a cone of blue lights flashing on his dashboard. André pulled up on the side of the road and switched off his engine. It seemed like an eternity as André sat in his car waiting for the policeman to get out of his car. André wondered what the policeman was doing; he certainly was not in any hurry. André figured that this was just a torture technique to get him stressed while he waited. André watched the side mirror and saw the policeman light up a cigarette and take a deep puff. Then as he blew out a long puff of smoke he got out of the car and adjusted his gun and baton on his leather belt. André quickly looked away and mentally prepared for this encounter.

The car shook momentarily as André heard the bang and then the sounds of falling chards of glass. André dared not move; he just sat there frozen. Piet Coetzee the policeman that had followed him came up to the driver's side window and with his baton tapped the window for André to open it. André rolled down the window and asked,

"What seems to be the problem, Officer?" Piet looked at André intently and said,

"May I see your driver's license?" André handed him his driver's license and again asked,

"Is everything OK?" Piet again looked at André intently and did not say anything for a long while. André was becoming uncomfortable with this and was becoming angry; the blood rushing to his face. Before André could blurt out his annoyance, Piet said,

"Your driver's side tail light is broken, please step out of the car". André opened his door and stepped out. He realized that his legs were weak and they were trembling. André had to support himself by holding onto the Toyota's roof. Piet did not miss that and he smiled as he saw the anguish in André's eyes. Piet starred at André and asked,

"Where are you coming from?" André decided to go along with this line of questioning and replied,

"I went to the hospital to visit my friend, but he was not there". Piet kicked at the gravel and a few stone chips hit André's shoes. Piet said looking at the dust on his highly polished boot,

"So you lost your friend. Do you know what it feels like to lose a friend permanently?" Piet waited briefly for an answer and not expecting to get one, he continued,

"You will find out and then you will know to stop meddling with those matters that do not concern you". Piet dropped André's driver's license onto the floor and kicked it under the Toyota. With a sneer he turned and walked back to his Ford Cortina. As he got into his car he shouted,

"Watch yourself now; you will never know who is watching you". Piet started his engine and roared away from the side of the road leaving André covered in a layer of dust.

It was a struggle, but André managed to retrieve his license from under his car. His hands and pants at the knees were dirty from kneeling on the floor and André just wanted to get home and wash up. As he drove home he realized that he was crying with rage and wiped his eyes. The thought that kept reverberating in his head was "You will find out and then you will know to stop meddling with those matters that do not concern you". "What did he mean with that statement?"

"Misty", the dog's image flashed through his mind. He had left the dog outside this morning when he left for the hospital and as he thought about it the hair on the back of his neck rose. Oh please no, not Misty.

CHAPTER 29

The evening air was unusually cool but André was sweating profusely while he dug a hole in his backyard. His tears burned as they rolled his hot cheeks and he found that he was pounding the ground with unnecessary force to break up the soil as he dug deeper and deeper. The force at which the shovel dug into the ground was fuelled by the intense rage he felt after he found Misty lying motionless on the ground.

He knew the dog was dead long before he picked her up. But he nevertheless rushed her to the veterinarian to see if he could save her. The veterinarian shook his head in empathy and said that the dog was obviously poisoned in the morning and had died several hours ago.

André kept repeating "Bastards, you bastards". He made a promise to Misty that they will pay for this. But André did not know who "they" were. It was the whole rotten system and he was no longer going to stand idly by because now it was personal. He was going to find Themba and fight for justice. André finished with the burial and said goodbye to his friend and companion. He went indoors and looked at the clock. It was fifteen minutes past eight in the evening and he had enough time to shower and clean up before it was time to call Dr Nirmal Ansari. If André had seen that white Ford Cortina in the street this evening he would have taken his shovel and bashed in the driver's head. It was fortunate for them that this evening they had decided to leave him alone with his misery.

Dr Ansari answered on the first ring as if he was sitting and waiting with his hands on the telephone handset. After they exchanged and established their identities Dr Ansari began with,

"May I call you André?" André quickly said "yes, please ". Dr Ansari continued,

"Please call me Nirmal, no need for formalities, you are amongst friends. André you are involved in a very serious cover up with that Zulu man that was shot by the police. I made some very discreet inquiries into what had happened after yesterday's incident". André cut in, now becoming anxious,

"What incident, what happened?" Nirmal Ansari continued as if he was reading from a book,

"The Zulu man regained consciousness and became agitated when he saw that he was restrained. He was subsequently knocked unconscious by one of the guards. I examined him a little later and he was fine. We had to stitch him up again as he tore some stitches in the struggle to get free. We received instructions to prepare him to be moved. The receiving destination was not given and we were told it was Security business. Later that day a private ambulance collected him and we were asked to provide them with all original documentation and any copies made".

André was intrigued, all that for Themba, a simple caring man. As if he read André's mind, Nirmal said,

"I became very suspicious. They were taking a lot of precautions for someone who they claim shot a policeman in a political unrest; so why the precautions for secrecy for a totally unknown mute Zulu man? So I made some inquires". Nirmal continued,

"I know some people at St Mary's hospital and one of the fellows there, a young Indian man by the name of Devraj was very helpful. He works in the hospital records and comes in contact with all the activities at that small hospital. Devraj told me that there were a lot of rumors at the time of the Harding massacre. One or two that were injured and escaped during the attack by the police were treated and released by St Mary's Hospital". Nirmal paused and said,

"What I am telling you can never be repeated and you cannot tell anyone how you came to know these things. I don't even know why I trust you. You are a White man and I could be risking my life. I guess I trust you because I saw how much you cared for that Zulu man and the risk you have taken to inquire about him. What is happening is wrong and if I am able to help him then I want to at least try". André started to assure Nirmal that he could trust him but he continued without waiting for affirmation of trust.

"Devraj said that the Zulu man who was shot by the police was seen as the village idiot. Apparently he was born with a defect larynx and could not speak. Devraj said that the man's name was Themba. He had made one of the girls at the village pregnant and when the baby was born he took the baby and ran away. It seems that the local Sangoma was planning to offer the baby as a sacrifice to appease the spirits of the forefathers. Devraj says that they were too scared to talk about why she wanted to sacrifice the baby especially now that the Sangoma was dead and her spirit watched over them". Nirmal took a deep breath and said,

"Now this is the really important part. Devraj says that from what he was able to piece together was; Themba took the baby and escaped from the village but ran into the Police patrol. Not being able to explain himself the police may have tried to arrest him and during the struggle he and the baby were shot. It appears that one of the policemen was also shot. He died at the scene. The baby also died but Themba survived the shooting. The policeman was shot with his own gun. The other policeman panicked and called the Riot Squad and things got out of hand. There was talk that there was someone else at the scene. That person ran back to the village and the Riot Squad followed him there. It was then that it got out of control. The massacre was unprovoked and many people died. There are some individuals in the police force at the Harding Police Station who want to portray this as a political uprising so as to hide the real truth."

Nirmal Ansari continued, "That is all I know, please take care of yourself and I wish you all the luck, God bless you for caring". André thanked him and hung the phone. André cautiously looked out of the window and was relieved that the street was empty. The white Ford Cortina was nowhere to be seen. André sat down and buried his head in his hands and prayed. He had lost his best friend, Misty. Themba was in deep trouble and he was at risk. He did not know what to do.

He reflected on his options and it seemed hopeless. The sharp ring of the phone made him jump. He looked at the phone as if it was going to attack him. He slowly got up and lifted the handset to his ears. After a minute of silence a voice said "Now you know how it feels like to lose a friend, don't meddle, leave things well alone". André opened his mouth to explode into the phone when he heard the dial tone. The caller had hung up the phone.

CHAPTER 30

That night André did not sleep at all. He was angry at what they did at the Zulu village and to his dog, he was sad to have lost his close friend and companion and he was scared for what they may do to him. All these emotions racked his mind and body at the same time and left him exhausted. He found that he was constantly checking the street throughout the night for that white Ford Cortina.

The next day he drove back to the hospital to visit Buhle. During his drive to the hospital he constantly checked his rearview mirror to see if he was being followed and to his relief there were no signs of that white Ford. By the time he had arrived at the hospital he was starting to relax and become complacent. André went up to the fourth floor and entered the woman's ward. Buhle was awake and was eating her breakfast when he arrived. He was pleased to see how much she had recovered although her eyes were swollen from crying.

As he had expected she asked for the baby and Themba. André was not able to tell her anymore than he knew the day before. He did however assure her that he was going to help Themba and find the baby. Buhle had heard about the massacre at the village from some of the patients in the ward. The news had distressed her tremendously. André spent the next hour or so talking with Buhle. She was very distressed to hear about what happened at the village and André had to comfort her several times. She cried openly for the great loss she suffered for the people that perished as these were folks she had grown up with and loved deeply. The hour that André spent with Buhle was one of the most heart wrenching times he had ever spent. He found that recently his life was filled with sorrow and he wondered when it was going to end. After promising to stay in touch with her André left the ward and made his way to the elevator. Several hospital staff and visitors were already in the elevator and André made his way to the back wall of the elevator just to get out of the way. He stood there with his head bowed deep in thought as he waited for the doors to close.

André did not see Nurse Lungile dive into the elevator as the doors were closing and she also made her way to the rear of the elevator and stood next to him. The elevator descended one floor and stopped. André was vaguely aware of the woman next to him shuffle and fight her way out from the rear to leave the elevator. As she did, she bumped against him and he felt a slight tug at his coat. He was a little annoyed that a person would enter an elevator and make their way to the rear and then fight their out at the next floor, bumping everyone. He figured that if you are planning to get off at one level from the one you entered then you should stay up front.

Getting off at the third floor Nurse Lungile saw Dr Ansari in the corridor. With a slight tilt of her head she acknowledged that her mission was successful. Nurse Lungile enjoyed the little diversion from her regular duties and especially felt special that Dr Ansari had trusted her. She did not think that Dr Ansari was as bad as the other nurses made him to be. She thought that he was kind and caring about his patients and demanded the best treatment for them.

André was still very pensive as he drove out of the hospital parking. Out of recent habit he looked in the rearview mirror to see if he was being followed. To his relief he did not see any vehicles behind him. He drove home to plan his next move. When he got home he parked his car on the street and walked up his driveway to his front door. As he did that he casually glanced up the street and he saw a small covered panel van parked some distance away. The van had a sign painted on it indicating that it belonged to a plumbing company. André figured that someone must have plumbing troubles and would not have thought anything of it but it seemed odd for two reasons. For one it was parked in the street. It is usual for these fix-it types of contractors to park on your driveway so that they have easy access to their tools and supplies. Secondly the van had a high powered antenna on the roof of the vehicle and that it did not fit the appearance of the vehicle. The windows were also tinted so that one could not see who was in it.

André entered his home and went into the kitchen to boil some water for a cup of tea. He sensed that there was something different in the house. André stood still for a moment but could not make sense of what he was feeling. He shook his head and said to himself that it was probably the fact that Misty was not around and the void in his life made him unsure of his surroundings. The hours crawled into late afternoon and darkness crept in. André had dozed in his comfortable recliner for most of the afternoon; his anguish over the recent days had taken a toll on him. The sound of his telephone jolted him out of his afternoon nap. He was sleeping so soundly that he had to orient himself before he answered the phone. As he became fully awake he was again struck with that strange feeling that something was different but could not figure out what it was. André picked up the phone and said,

"This is André, may I help you". The voice on the other end said,

"Hello André, this is Nirmal at the hospital. Did you get the note I sent you? We are making progress. I will continue to make inquires and hopefully get to the bottom of what happened at that Harding massacre. Please let me know what you find out after you read my note". André was confused as he wondered, "What note?" And then he remembered the interaction at the elevator and now he recalled subconsciously that the person that brushed alongside him was Nurse Lungile. It now made sense. "She must have slipped a note into his jacket pocket when she bumped into him", he thought.

"Hello, hello, are you there André?" came the concerned voice of Dr Nirmal Ansari. André embarrassed by not being aware of the subterfuge engineered by the good doctor, quickly said,

"Oh yes, I am here, yes I will let you know soon" and then thanked the doctor for his help. Nirmal wished André the best of luck and hung up the phone. André still had the phone to his ear as he replayed the events in that elevator. There was a dead silence on the phone and André was about to put it down when he heard a distinct click on the line and then he heard a busy dial tone. André thought that was strange, it was as if there was someone else on the line. Now two things bothered him. One was the unusual quiet stillness of the house and the other was the click on the phone.

As he thought those thoughts, it hit him. The quiet stillness of the house, why was it so quiet? He could always hear the traffic as background sound from a nearby freeway and he was used to it. Now as he listened he could not hear it. That was what had bothered him; he did not have that background sound of traffic. It was too quiet.

He got up and went to the kitchen and looked around. Knowing what he was looking for, he was able to spot it immediately. The kitchen door that lead to the sun room at the rear of the house was closed shut.

The sun room was the room that Misty always used to sleep in as it was cool. The room had half height walls with nylon mesh instead of windows. It was protected from the rain by low hanging awnings. André never completely closed that door as Misty would come into the house through that door when he needed to. For years he had left that door slightly ajar and never closed it and since the neighborhood was safe it was not an issue to leave it open and unlocked. He remembered that this morning he had seen it ajar slightly and left it that way out of habit. The door was heavy and the wind never moved it, so why was it closed now? Some one had closed that door this morning and he knew that it was not him.

A feeling of dread crept into him and his hands suddenly felt clammy. He looked at the stairways that led to his utility room and instinctively grabbed a hockey stick from his closet. Should he go down there? Memories of Misty came flooding back and rage filled his heart. He turned on the light in the stairway and taking a firm hold of the hockey stick he descended down the stairs. He had a feeling that someone had gone down these stairs recently as the dust and cobwebs were disturbed.

When André reached the bottom he found to his relief that the small room was empty. He looked around and noticed that the dust had been disturbed at one corner of the room. André went to the corner and saw a small grey box mounted to the wall near his telephone junction terminals. The small grey box had an antenna attached to it. Coming out of the box were two wires that were crudely connected to the existing telephone junction box. André was not an expert in electronic devices but he knew enough to figure out that this box spliced into his telephone line was listening in to his telephone calls and was transmitting to a nearby receiver. Leaving everything intact André went back upstairs and peered through his window. The panel van was still parked in the street and it was now joined by another vehicle, a white Ford Cortina.

CHAPTER 31

André watched the two vehicles on his street and a cold dread came over him. They heard his last conversation with Dr Nirmal Ansari. He suddenly became afraid for Dr Ansari. He needed to warn him but how? He could not call him since the phone is monitored. He needed to get to a public phone and make the call; he could not afford to wait longer. André considered his options. He had to leave his house unseen and hide out at his cabin in the hills. Very few people knew he had that cabin and those that did, had no knowledge where it was. It was his secret getaway place and he had gone to a lot of trouble in keeping it a secret.

First he needed to see the note that Dr Ansari had written. André went to the coat closet and fished around in his pocket. He found the note and read,

"We have found where they have taken Themba. Devraj has been very helpful. He discreetly used his networking contacts in the records department and found that Themba was taken to Berea a suburb of Durban and placed in a private ward at St Andrews Hospital. Themba was heavily sedated and is not a flight risk. It is expected that he would be there until his trial comes up. I found out from other sources that the trial is imminent and they are looking to convict him for murder and treason. The judge will most likely hand down a death sentence. They want to do this with no publicity. I know that you will help him; God bless and protect you"

The gravity of Themba's situation struck André hard. He sat down to wrestle with his thoughts. Nirmal mentioned "no publicity" and that struck a chord with him. He remembered the reporter that wrote the article on the Harding massacre as he was a very controversial writer and usually choose to write editorials for the newspaper that were highly emotional. André remembered that his name was James Anderson and that he wrote for the South Coast Times. André knew now what he needed to do. He packed a small bag and gathered all the money in cash that he had at home.

His late wife's sister by the name of Norma was a feisty woman who did not take nonsense from anyone. She was very supportive when André lost his wife in that tragic accident and promised to help him if he needed it. Now was the time to call in those favors. Without hesitation he called her number and as it rang he heard the soft click on the line. André would have missed it if he was not listening for it. After a couple of rings Norma picked up the phone and with a confident voice said'

"Hello, may I help you". André was relieved that she did not give her name. He said quickly'

"I need to talk to you this evening, can you come over?" Norma was concerned and said'

"You mean now?" André again quickly cut in before Norma said too much,

"Yes please, now. Misty died yesterday. He was sick. I am rather distressed and need someone to talk to". Norma sensing that not all is well and being a woman of action she did not want to waste time on the phone. She said,

"I will be there soon, set a cup of tea for me".

Within thirty minutes, Norma had driven up André's driveway and was at his front door. André was glad that he had parked on the street which allowed Norma to come all the way up the driveway. André let the very concerned Norma into the house and put his finger to his lips to silence her. Norma was confused but decided to play along. André walked her out to the backyard and took her to Misty's grave. He did not want to talk in the house just in case it was also bugged. He wanted to focus his interaction with Norma around the dog just in case he was being watched. Standing by Misty's grave, André calmly told Norma everything that transpired, leaving nothing out. As André explained the sequence of events Norma became increasingly angry and when he was done, she was ready to get revenge.

Within half an hour Norma made a point of saying goodbye as she exited the front door and keeping her head away from the parked vehicles on the street she opened the driver's side door and got in. When she got in she turned off the car's interior dome light. On cue André crouching at the side of the garage quickly moved to the car; his body bent over so that he could not be seen by the people in the two vehicles on the street. He opened the rear door and slipped into the floor of the back seat. He gently pulled the car door shut as Norma started the engine to muffle the sound.

The men in the parked vehicles strained their eyes to see who the driver was but Norma was moving too quickly away from them for them to make out her face. Norma turned on her headlight only when she was half away out of the street. The men in the parked vehicles had hoped that they had chosen a spot on the other side of André's house so that that car would have to pass them on its way out. They however were not too concerned as it was their job to watch André and not his female guests.

Norma drove André to her home to pick up some supplies for his cabin and when he got there he made a dash for the phone. He dialed Dr Nirmal Ansari and waited nervously for the doctor to answer. After several rings a female voice answered,

"This is the Ansari's residence". It was a confident voice and André assumed that it was the doctor's wife. André blurted out,

"May I speak to Nirmal please it is an emergency". The woman on the phone did not react to the urgency as she was used to getting such calls for the doctor. Without changing her tone, she said,

"Dr Ansari just left the house. He was called to the hospital for an emergency; you can reach him there in twenty minutes from now". André winced as if he was punched in the stomach, but realizing that he was over reacting, he said,

"Thank you, I am sorry to bother you" and hung up the phone. André couldn't shake the feeling he had inside of him. He was worried for the doctor's safety. There was nothing he could do right now, so decided to wait for the morning.

Norma let André take her car and he headed to the security of his cabin in the hills. Secure in his cabin, André slept like a baby. He had always enjoyed this cabin and the fresh air invigorated him. He was boiling water for his coffee when he heard the sound of a car coming up the hill. It was at least five miles away he figured as sound traveled long distances up here. That is the reason he felt secure here as no one can sneak up on him. He watched the dirt road for a while and saw that it was Norma's spare car and André relaxed. It took at least another five minutes before that car drove up to André's cabin.

André went up to greet Norma as she stepped out holding the morning news paper. André noticed that she was not her usual feisty manner. Her shoulders were drooped and she had a sullen look on her face. André went up to her and said,

"Good morning Norma, is everything OK?" Norma did not look directly at André and softly said,

"I am sorry André, we will get those bastards", and handed André a copy of the South Coast Times, a local morning news paper. André tried to strop the tremble in his hands as he held the paper up to read, but the dread he felt just made it worse. His chest muscles tightened and he suddenly felt the cool morning air stifle him. On the front page was the headline,

"Doctor drowns himself at the Port Sheptone Beach". With a sinking feeling André read the report that followed.

"Police were summoned to the Port Sheptone Beach at one o'clock in the morning when some campers reported that a body had washed ashore by the incoming tide. Piet Coetzee from the Harding police reported that this looked like a suicide drowning and not a robbery as the Doctor was fully clothed and still had his wallet on him. Evidence of bruising on his face and body indicated that the doctor's body was thrown against the rocks in the rough seas before being washed up on the beach. The doctor's grief stricken wife, positively identified him as Dr Nirmal Ansari."

André could not read anymore. He sank to his knees and wailed like a wounded animal. Norma came to him and held him as she would a little child. After a few minutes André stood up and using his shirt sleeves he wiped the tears from his eyes. His eyes blazed against the morning light and there was such intensity in them that Norma caught her breath in surprise. Speaking with determination André said with clenched teeth,

"They have gone too far this time; I am going to get even. Did you manage to get the phone number of that reporter, James Anderson?"

CHAPTER 32

Commander Villiers was a large bulky man with piercing blue eyes. When he spoke his voice filled the room and drowned every other sound. He commanded the respect of his riot squad and it was a well known fact that he ran the local police station although he was not the station commander. Commander Villiers also was well networked and had friends in the ranks of the Justice Department all the way to the Minister of Justice. He earned his favor by carrying out successfully many clandestine assignments against individuals of all nationalities that were a threat to the White Government.

Commander Villiers had spent the last few minutes dressing down Constable Piet Coetzee for his incompetence and now he stood there and just stared at the constable. Piet recoiled at the verbal onslaught and now he tried to look away but the Commander's glare held Piet's eyes in a hypnotic bondage. At last the Commander spoke breaking the stare and Piet slumped down in his chair,

"So you lost André Pretorius. He slipped through your fingers, right under your nose. And you killed the doctor before he could tell you who his sources were. You incompetent idiot, did you do anything right?"

Piet nodded apologetically to those rhetorical questions. He wanted to add that the doctor refused to give up names and they needed to turn up the heat. But then the doctor died unexpectedly when he received a blow to the side of his head. Piet stopped short of making excuses as he knew that was not what the Commander wanted to hear. The Commander continued as if he needed to convince himself,

"What we did that night was for our fatherland. Some of them that were killed in the village were teenagers, but they would become terrorists later. We are doing what we had to do to manage the uprisings. So if some women and children were killed then it was just too bad. It is a battle zone out there and we have to protect ourselves. We are protecting our country for the future, for our children and our children's children. If we let any one of these terrorists get away with anything then there will be no end to the uprisings. The Blacks have their own homelands, we gave them that. They should stay in their own homelands and leave us alone. Next thing they will demand is to take over the country. Over my dead body, I tell you, over my dead body".

Snapping out of his trance, he became aware that Piet was still in the room and was watching him. Regaining his composure, he turned to Piet and with a determination that Piet had never seen before, Commander Villiers said,

"Find André and detain him. Keep it quiet. I want you to extract from him everything he knows. Do not leave any marks on his body. Use the sand filled stocking and the invisible chair, it works very well. He will break sooner or later".

Piet shuddered at the mention of the invisible chair. It was a form of torture that was commonly used to break a prisoner down. The prisoner is asked to sit on an invisible chair until his muscles cramp up in trying to support him in this position. If the prisoner falls to the ground he is beaten with a stocking filled with sea sand. The blows to the body were transmitted to the organs inside the body and left very little bruising on the outside. The pain from the cramping muscles endured from the invisible chair treatment was so severe that the thought of repeating the exercise was enough to make the prisoner pliable and willing to cooperate. Piet nodded that he understood and got up to leave. The Commander put is hand on Piet's shoulder and said quietly,

"Don't fail me this time". A hint of a smile creased the Commander's face for a moment and Piet felt its message. Piet nodded and strode out of the room.

Commander Villiers waited until Piet had left the office and then went to his desk and picked up the phone. He dialed a number and waited for the call to be answered. After a few short rings the call was answered. The Commander spoke softly in to the mouthpiece,

"How soon can you arrange a trial to convict that mute for treason against our Government and for the shooting death of Johan?" The smile that crept onto the Commander's face was affirmation that the response was to his liking. The Commander continued with renewed enthusiasm,

"This should be a straight forward case. He killed a police officer who was on duty investigating an uprising. The mute was the leader of the uprising that subsequently had to be crushed by the riot squad. If this is not a classic case for death by hanging then I don't know what is. Let's speed it up before the newspaper gets wind of the story and we would have to deal with the bleeding Progressive Party liberals. Since we do not have jury trials in this country we should be able to railroad this through the court relatively easily. I want this "Harding massacre" episode to go away quietly with no publicity especially after the exposure of the death of Steve Biko recently".

Commander Villiers caught himself; he just referred to the incident at the village as the "Harding massacre". He had to be careful and not do that again. He cannot view that incident as a police massacre. He said aloud, "Damm that reporter, Anderson, for writing that column and calling it the Harding massacre". Now the public has a handle to hold on to. By giving it a name he had given it life and it can grow out of control. The Commander would have preferred to call it an incident that would soon be forgotten. He wanted this incident forgotten as soon as possible. Realizing that the Judge was still on the line, the Commander said,

"Thank you for moving up the case so quickly. He has recovered from his injuries, but we have him sedated to keep him under control".

After exchanging some pleasantries, Commander Villiers gently placed the receiver on its cradle and stretched back on his office chair, his muscles relaxing for the first time this morning. He knew that he was sitting on a landmine and it could blow up at anytime. He looked out of the window and thought about leaving South Africa for the first time, but as he reflected on leaving the country he wondered, where else could he and his family live so comfortably. The weather was great; they had a nice house in a wealthy neighborhood. He had a maid and gardener who lived in the servant's quarters on the premises. His children went to a private school and they lived a comfortable life with Church on Sundays. Why would he want to change that, he was not going to let them take his country and life style away from him.

There was a knock on the door and the Commander barked "come in". A neatly dressed Black Zulu girl walked in with a tray containing a pot of steaming hot tea and a cup. Also on the tray sat a small plate of Marie biscuits, his favorite. She greeted the Commander with a smile and a pleasant "Good Morning Sir" in strongly accented English. She placed the tray on the side table and then placed the morning newspaper that she was carrying under her arm, along side the tea tray. She then politely left the room.

The Commander picked up the newspaper and proceeded to the sports page. As he scanned the insides of the paper his eyes focused on a column written by James Anderson. The Commander's pulse quickened; he needed to do something about that reporter as he was starting to become a thorn in his side. With that thought in mind he picked up his phone and called a number he knew by heart.

CHAPTER 33

In a side street on the outskirts of Port Shepstone a white Ford Cortina had parked under a large tree that provided shade as well as some cover for his prying eyes. The two occupants of the car became suddenly alert after sitting in the car for several hours. A late model blue Honda Accord just drove into the covered parking of the high rise apartment complex they were watching. One of them took out a note pad and wrote the date and time down as they watched James Anderson exit his car, lock the car doors and make his way to the elevator. James was a slim man in his late thirties with boyish features. James lived alone in a corner apartment on the second floor of this apartment complex. The men in the parked car could see James exit the elevator that was located to the right of his apartment and make his way to his corner apartment. The men relaxed again; their orders were to just monitor James and identify and document anyone he meets with.

James saw from the corner of his eye the white car parked in the street. As a reporter he was trained to notice details like that. His conversation with his editor this afternoon came rushing back to him. His editor had called him in to his office and while discussing the late edition of the paper he whispered to James that he should be careful. The editor cautiously warned him that he has being placed under watch by the SB. The SB was an acronym for "Security Branch" a much feared Government security organization. This did not scare James and he figured that there was obviously something going on that involves him and that just meant more news worthy scoop. James had to be cautious however as his only protection was his public image and reader following. This did not protect him from accidental drowning or an unfortunate accident on the freeway. James had however one thing in his favor, he was a seasoned reporter and had played this cat and mouse game with the SB before and had walked circles around them. He loved the challenge.

The afternoon sun created a perfect backdrop for the fortunate ones who could take the time to enjoy an afternoon cup of tea at the local café in an all White suburb of Port Shepstone. Idly chatting in one shady corner of the patio of this café sat three middle aged women. To the casual observer these were three middle-aged bored housewives enjoying an afternoon tea and biscuits. The casual observer would have been fooled.

At the table sat Norma, André and James Anderson. They had arrived separately and there was some curious interest from some of the patrons when André walked in disguised as a woman in woman's clothing and a wig. The patrons saw André as an aging woman who seriously needed a dose of estrogen. In a low voice James said,

"Please call me Jean while I am in this disguise" and then proceeded to explain how this evolved.

"My Dad was a carpenter and he was a very good one at that. He had many ideas of how to circumvent problems. He has since passed on but while he was alive we worked·on this scheme together. We needed a way for me to move around undetected so we found this apartment that I presently live in. Since it was a newly built complex the adjoining apartment was also available. My Dad looked at it from its logistics point of view and decided that it would be perfect. He bought that adjoining apartment under his Aunt's name. My Dad then found where the closets of both apartments shared a common wall and very cleverly constructed a door way between both apartments through their respective closets. The doorway was very well hidden and unless you knew where to look you would never find it during a search.

The entrance to that second apartment faces the rear of the complex and is serviced by an elevator and corridor at the rear of the building. So when I need to be invisible as James Anderson all I do is go into my apartment and enter the adjoining apartment through the closet. In that apartment I have all these woman's clothing and special makeup and a blonde wig. It takes a while to change characters but I have become good at it over the years. I leave through the adjoining apartment and use a second car that is parked at the rear. I often will pass the surveillance guys and they will give me an admiring look". Flicking the hair of his blonde wig, James said,

"I think I make quite a good looking blonde". With that remark, James smiled broadly and said,

"The only problem is when I need to go to the toilet, it can be embarrassing". James continued as the other two watched with amazement on how well James has adapted to his female role. Norma spoke first,

"It took a lot of convincing to have André dress into female clothing, but I talked him into it. It was rather fun to do his make up". André who was uncomfortable in woman's clothing and makeup shifted uncomfortably in his seat. He wanted this charade to be over with quickly. He did not look as attractive as James did in woman's clothing but was sure that the looks he got when he walked into the café was because of his walk. James sensing André s discomfort said,

"Why don't you start at the beginning and tell me everything and we can go from there?"

James nodded as he listened intently. André gave every detail and even stopped to wipe a tear from his eyes when he mentioned Misty's untimely death. Norma's heart went to André as she saw him try to wipe his tears with his blouse sleeve in a most un-womanly way and she quickly offered him a Kleenex tissue from her purse.

When André had finished telling him his story, James sat there for a long moment not saying a word. And then he spoke,

"I am truly sorry for the losses you have suffered. It is unfortunate that we have to live with this type of abuse and injustice. To put things in perspective consider these facts".

James looked pensive as he reached into his memory banks for statistics that have haunted him for a long time. He continued,

"This country is reputed to have one of the highest rates of judicial executions in the world. About one thousand people in the last ten years alone were executed and ninety five percent of that were Black South Africans. Studies have shown that the death penalty was far more likely to be imposed if the victim of a capital offence was white and the perpetrator was black".

James looked at André for reaction but all he saw was André's face drop with despair. James continued,

"Defying the Geneva Convention, capital punishment was also used against those found guilty of political offences, although South Africa was a signatory to the nineteen forty nine convention. However as another statement of defiance, South Africa had declined to sign the nineteen seventy seven addenda extending the definition of prisoner of war to captured guerrillas".

André's face dropped even more with despair. James continued,

"We have to make sure that we keep Buhle away from Themba for now as her life may be in danger if the SB makes a connection between them. Do not contact her or make any inquiries about her for now. You need to lie low for a while. I will make some inquiries regarding Themba and then we shall act". James looked grave; he had to make sure that there were no false expectations.

"I have to level with you" James said quietly.

"It does not look good for Themba" James said raising his left hand. Using his right hand he started to count on his fingers the number of factors that were against Themba.

"Firstly, Themba is a Black adult male. He is a Black male who killed a White male. He is a Black male who killed a White policeman. He is a Black male who is portrayed as an enemy of the State. All these individually will certainly get him a death sentence by hanging and he cannot defend himself because of his speech impediment". Hearing James go through the factors one by one made Themba look like a really bad person. He knew for sure the Judge will not be sympathetic.

"And the baby" James continued "dies in the confrontation". If that is brought out then Themba will also be seen as a baby killer. There will not be any public sympathy for him. We will need to keep the baby's death out of the picture. After all there is nothing we can do; the baby is dead, buried in the mass grave with the others."

"If you need to contact me, call the South Coast Times office at Port Shepstone and ask for the cafeteria. When you are connected to the cafeteria ask for Jean. Who ever answers in the cafeteria will tell you that there is no one by that name and then you say that is Ok and hang up. I will get the message. Do not call my apartment, if you want to stay alive". As Norma and André got up to leave, James looked at them and saw their dissolute figures make their way out of the patio. They looked beaten and yet they came to him with so much of hope. James got up and followed them to their car. He said in a comforting voice,

"I will do everything that I can possibly do to save him"

CHAPTER 34

With tear filled eyes, Meena Ansari sat at her kitchen table and watched the birds come and feed at her bird feeder. They were so care free and she hoped that she could sprout wings and fly off into the open sky away from all this misery. Meena had met Nirmal Ansari when he was an intern at a hospital in Durban where she had worked as a registered nurse. Meena was an attractive tall Indian woman with long black hair that she always wore loosely down her back. Although she was perceived as being quiet and shy, Nirmal found her to be a strong woman with quiet determination. That was probably why he was attracted to her as she was a pillar of strength to him. They were meant for each other and after a whirlwind romance they married and moved about a hundred miles south to the coast town of Port Shepstone. Meena had given up her career as a nurse because she wanted to stay at home and raise a family. It was too late now, she never had a chance. He was gone out of life forever, but memories of him kept her from falling apart.

Meena did not know who to be angry with. She was always concerned with Nirmal's stance against the apartheid policies, especially when he was at medical school. Should she be angry with the Government for she was not sure whether or not it was an act of one person working without the Government's consent or Government policy being enforced? Nirmal had a passion for justice and Meena seemed to be compelled by his determination to seek justice regardless of the consequences. She dried her eyes and now filled with the same determination she got up from her kitchen table and went into her bedroom. There she spotted that cedar chest with its secret compartment at the bottom. Her heart leaped at the thought of what she was about to do. For the first time after Nirmal's death she felt alive and full of purpose.

The café at the outskirts of Port Shepstone was once again home to the ladies with an impossible mission. Meena had contacted Nurse Lungile who in turn talked to Buhle and finally they got word to André and James Anderson. Norma played host to the group and sat at the head of the table. Next to her sat André. He was starting to look a little more comfortable in woman's clothing. Flanked on his right was Jean, the alter ego of James Anderson the reporter. Meena sat opposite all of them, looking attractive in her traditional Indian garments. Her renewed determination had brought the color back to her cheeks and her glowed with intensity.

Meena leaned forward and said,

"My husband was passionate about justice and equal treatment of all nationalities. He wanted to establish himself as Doctor and then work to dismantle the apartheid policies." André wondered how this was going to help Themba now but waited patiently to hear what she had to say.

"My husband is dead", she continued, "but I want to bring justice to the person or person's who killed him". She paused to take a sip of hot tea. She continued,

"My husband would want me to do this. He had prepared for the time when he might have to go in to exile. Now he does not have to worry about that. He had accumulated and hidden a large sum of money for an emergency escape. I want to use this money to help Buhle and Themba fight this injustice". Reaching down to her side, she picked up a medium sized leather case and placed it on the table, pushing it forward to André. André looked at Norma and James for approval to accept the case and they both nodded back at him. André opened the latches of the leather case and carefully peeked in side it as if he was expecting something to jump out at him. His eyes widened as he saw the neatly bound and stacked South African Rand bank notes inside. Meena said as a matter of fact,

"There is about fifty thousand South African Rands in there. Please use it to avenge my husband's death and to help Buhle and Themba. I am willing to help in the struggle so please feel free to contact me. You may reach me through Nurse Lungile."

There was no reason to question her resolve. The group at the table thanked her for her generosity and welcomed her to their quest for freedom and justice. The core group now grew by one member, each nationality being represented, fighting for a common cause.

The struggle she felt inside her to get justice for her late husband was obviously taking its toll on her. A tear rolled down her cheek and she graciously brushed it aside and not allowing her emotions to weaken her composure, she said,

"There is more money available if you need it", and with that she stood up elegantly and turned to walk away. The men at the table dressed as women looked at this elegant woman admiringly as she walked away. The one true woman at the table also looked her admiringly as she strode away, both sexes admiringly her differently. James was the first to speak breaking the spell that had them mesmerized.

"We have to get Buhle to Durban and have her see Themba to calm him down. The private hospital that they are keeping him in is on the same network as St Mary's Hospital at Harding. Our contact at St Mary's is an Indian man who is the records clerk there and goes by the name of Devraj. He has been very helpful to the late Dr Ansari. He was the person who found the location where they moved Themba to. Devraj has been monitoring the records of Themba and will let us know if any change is imminent. Devraj says that they are keeping Themba sedated until the trial."

Norma cut in, "Nurse Lungile said that Buhle has recovered and will be released any day now. Nurse Lungile has volunteered to have Buhle move in with her parents in Umlazi which is on the south side of Durban. Buhle can travel easily by bus to the private hospital in Berea, a suburb of Durban. Once Buhle is out of hospital she will drop out of the SB's radar and they will forget she even existed".

André added, "We initiated a search for the baby. Devraj has been very helpful, once again. He did a search in the hospital records for any Black baby that was brought in the night of the massacre and no records were found. He did the same search at the other nearby hospitals and did not find any records." André could not have known that Devraj had included in his search criteria for a Black baby. In fact if he left that match criteria blank he would have found an Indian baby admitted on the night of the massacre.

André's face went dark; he said softly, "As hard as it is to accept, we have to admit to ourselves that the baby had perished during the massacre and is buried in that mass grave. We have to move on and save the living". As if to break the cold chains of despair, Norma said with renewed enthusiasm,

"I have a plan; I know what we can do to get Themba out of trouble. James, we will need your help". James looked up at Norma and nodded.

Norma continued, "André you will be the first to lay the ground work for Themba. That will mean you will have to enter the lion's den to accomplish that" and saying that she looked at André to see his resolve. André was steadfast in his commitment for Themba. Satisfied that she could count on André, Norma continued,

"The girls can play a crucial role here. It is going to be dangerous for them; in fact it is going to be dangerous for all of us if we get caught. God help us to succeed."

Norma still excited said, "We are going to need Meena for this as well, but not for her money". André and James were intrigued by Norma's enthusiasm and energy as she unfolded her plan to save Themba from hanging.

CHAPTER 35

The St Andrews private hospital in Berea, south of the city of Durban was located off the main road in a heavily wooded area. The location was deliberate for the hospital catered to the wealthy White patients who were admitted for treatment that required a long term stay. Since this area was zoned for White South Africans, the hospital did not admit non-White patients. If a non-White patient required admittance in extraordinary circumstances then the patient had to seek permission from the Minister of Home Affairs. If permission was granted, it was done so with conditions. In these extremely rare occasions, the patient had to be admitted to a private wing of the hospital with a private bath and toilet facilities. There could be no opportunities for the different nationalities to mix. In these cases the patient must also bear the cost of these private quarters. This however did not apply to the Security Forces who on request for holding a patient under guard were always granted access to the private quarters. The hospital had conveniently built a private wing to the hospital with additional alternate entrances so that one may come and go without distressing the other White patients at the hospital.

It was in this wing that the SB held the sedated prisoner, known only as "Political Prisoner number 1921". The covert identity was deliberate since the record keeping in the hospital system was not necessarily secure. It was this weakness in the security system that Devraj had exploited to gain access and obtain information on the transfer of Themba from the Provincial hospital in Harding to St Andrews in Berea. It was easy for Devraj to match the date of departure and the date of admission and then look for anonymous names in the systems. Devraj then monitored all the drugs and medical treatments that were administered to Themba daily and from that he was able to monitor the health of Themba. On a daily basis he fed the information to Lungile and Buhle and that was then transmitted to Norma who monitored the whole operation.

André and Norma moved their locations to separate apartments in the city of Durban. Meena also moved to an apartment in Durban after leaving unclear false information with neighbors and friends that she needed to get away for a while and that she was going to spend some time with friends in Cape Town. James Anderson remained in Port Shepstone and watched the guards waste their time watching empty houses in the wrong city. James had his assignment and he needed to be close to his office in Port Shepstone to be effective.

Their surveillance combined with information from inside sources at St Andrews confirmed that there were two guards at any one time and when they changed shifts. They were ready to execute their plan that had only one chance to be successful.

That morning was no different to most mornings at St Andrews Hospital. The guards were already on duty since six in the morning. They were assigned from a local police station and were given very little information about the prisoner, except that he was very dangerous and cannot be allowed to escape. They were given only one number to call in case of emergencies with this prisoner and that was to Commander Villiers. That number was to be used twenty fours a day, with no exceptions. The reputation of Commander Villiers was sufficient to instill absolute terror in the guards for failing to carry out simple instructions.

At ten in the morning the guards stiffened and stood to attention as they heard footsteps come along the long corridor to the deserted wing of the hospital. They were expecting the doctor and nurse at this time in the morning to do their regular check up but they were a little surprised to see two nurses accompany the doctor. As they got closer the guards looked at them curiously expecting some kind of explanation.

André dressed in a white lab coat with a stethoscope over his shoulder led the pack. He carried a small medical bag and the glasses he wore combined with a stick-on moustache gave him a completely different look. He also had two inserts placed inside both sides of his mouth between his cheeks and his teeth. These cheek inserts, with help from James Anderson made his face fuller and gave him a much younger look. It also changed the way he spoke. André was of the opinion that even his own mother would not have recognized him. This gave him a sense of security and as a result he walked upright and confident.

Meena was on his left dressed in a nurse's uniform, with her long black hair tied tightly into a bun and hidden under a nurse's cap. Her makeup and nurses dress was carefully crafted by Norma so that it de-emphasized her face by the way it was applied and emphasized her shapely body by the way it showed off her cleavage and long legs. When the guard's looked at her they had difficulty raising their eyes above her chest and had to force them selves to look at André instead.

Norma also did her magic with Buhle who was dressed to show off her curvy lines and abundant breasts. Buhle had lost almost all of the extra weight she had gained throughout her pregnancy and her recent medical condition also helped. Her dazzling smile and bright eyes disarmed the guards and made them a little vulnerable. Both Buhle and Meena were enjoying their new found power as they would not ordinarily dress this way and use their assets for personal benefit. André felt confident that he could talk his way past these guards since he was armed with these two women on either side of him. André spoke without being challenged,

"Today the patient is due for his bed bath and a new sleeping position. If we do not take care of that he will develop bed sores. These bed sores can be quite disgusting when they become infected; they ooze blood and yellow fluid". André made a disgusted face and sent the visual of what might be, directly across to the guards. Still twisting his face in disgust, André said,

"I will increase his sedative while we work on him but I will need you to unlock his handcuff hands one at a time as we bathe him". Watching the guard's hesitation, André quickly said,

"Off course, I will understand if you don't want to get all that blood and fluid on your clean uniform and just let us do it. I don't think he has any communicable diseases, but then we don't know his history. We will wear gloves, but sometimes the blood just spatters". André smiled inside when he saw the guard suddenly turn green and swallow quickly to stop himself from wrenching. The guard not wanting to let the doctor think he was getting away with any thing, said in a firm voice,

"OK here is the key, but no funny stuff. We will be outside when you are done and you can return the key then. If we suspect any thing we will come in shooting and you will die along with the patient. Do you understand?" André and the two women nodded their heads in feigned submission and this pleased the guards. They took the keys from the guard and entered the hospital room where Themba slept, closing the door behind them. The guards positioned themselves in the corridor, alert to any activity that was suspicious.

CHAPTER 36

Buhle gasped when she saw Themba lying on the bed. He looked so helpless and her heart went out to him. Themba lay with one hand handcuffed to the bed frame and on the other arm he had an IV drip attached to it. His bruises were healed and besides the fact that he was sedated, Themba was OK. André speaking to Buhle said,

"Quickly use the keys and unlock his handcuff we don't have much time. Then find the keys that look alike in the medical bag we brought with us and remember to hand those keys back to the guard when we leave. Keep the guard's keys safely."

Meena was busy preparing the syringe that contained the drug that would counter act the sedative that was being administered to Themba through his IV. From the Hospital records Devraj provided the name and concentration of the sedative that was being administered to Themba. Meena worked discreetly with her anesthetist resources at the Provincial hospital and obtained the counter drug to this sedative. She went over to Themba and injected the recommended dosage into his arteries.

The three of them watched Themba nervously, for what seemed like an eternity although it was only a few minutes. They were concerned that he would come out of his sedated state confused and become agitated. Meena was ready with the sedative just in case they needed it to put him under again. Themba stirred in his sleep and his breathing became deeper as he slowly recovered from his unconscious state. He opened his eyes slowly and took in the scene around him. He had not fully regained consciousness and he was still dazed. His eyes scanned the room and he focused on Buhle. There was a sudden recognition and his eyes brightened almost instantly.

Buhle put a finger to Themba's lips and signaled him to be quiet. Tears rolled down Themba's cheek as his eyes told her that the baby was dead. Buhle understood his grief and she gently kissed him on the lips and whispered,

"I know Themba; I know that you had done everything possible to protect the baby. The most important thing is that you are alive". Buhle continued, not waiting for Themba to react,

"Themba, promise me that you will stay calm. We are here to help you get out of this room". Themba for the first time became aware that there were others in the room. He focused on André and his heart warmed at the sight of his smiling face. It did however take him a little while to recognize André with his glasses and moustache. André spoke softly,

"Themba we will help you but you need to listen carefully. This is Meena, who is also here to help you. We have unlocked your handcuffs and we will leave the key with you. When we leave you, we will put the handcuffs back on. Meena will replace the IV with normal saline solution so that you will not be drugged, but we want you to pretend that you are asleep until this evening." André looked at Themba earnestly to see whether he understood what was happening. André was pleased to see Themba attentive and he seemed to understand so far. André continued,

"We noticed that the guard keeps his Thermos flask on that table" pointing to a Thermos flask on the stainless steel table across the room.

André said, "Meena is going to add a very potent sedative into that flask of coffee. During our watch over the past couple of days we noticed that both guards drank coffee out of the same Thermos at around four in the afternoon. The drug will put them to sleep in about two hours. We will monitor them from that tall building opposite this hospital. When we feel that they are asleep then we will come and get you. In the meantime you must prepare yourself to leave by unlocking the handcuffs and dressing up with the clothes we brought you. We will leave the clothes in the closet located in your private bathroom." André saw that Themba understood so far and he was proud of how well he was handling this sudden change of plans. Buhle also stood and admired this man, her Themba. Meena had just finished adding the drug to the flask and after shaking it set it down.

André from his surveillance knew that the entrance to this wing of the hospital is secluded and leads to a side street that is deserted. He also knew that the gate stays locked and can only be opened from the inside, so he will somehow have to make arrangements to make it stay unlocked when they leave. Since the gate is not in the guards view he could sneak around the side of the building and prop it open. The guards never checked that gate in the past days, so he did not expect them to check tonight.

"I will press the car's hooter for two short blasts to let you know that you should start dressing and that we are coming to get you". André said looking at Themba. He was relieved to see that Themba was still attentive and alert. Themba nodded his head periodically to indicate that he understood what was said so far.

André continued, "The guards may come in to check on you so keep the handcuffs locked and the key safely tucked away from their view. Don't let them know that you are conscious. Do you understand everything you have to do?" Themba nodded in acknowledgement. André gathered his things in preparation to leave. Buhle leaned over and kissed Themba on the lips and said that she will wait for him tonight. As she patted down the bed covers, the door flew open and one of the guards stepped in and barked,

"Are you finished yet? What is taking you so long?" The three of them jumped at the sudden intrusion but regained their composure quickly.

"We were just finishing up, so he is all yours" André said quickly and nudged Buhle to give him the keys. Buhle handed him the keys and proceeded to leave the room. The guard looked at the keys and then at Themba, focusing on his wrist. He went over to Themba, who by now was lay perfectly still, feigning unconsciousness. The guard tugged at the handcuff to make sure it was secure. He decided to unlock it and transfer the cuffs to the other hand and fingered the keys to insert it into the handcuff lock. Buhle held her breath in anguished anticipation. Themba stiffened.

André blurted out, "Sergeant, you need to put some gloves on when you touch him. Remember, we do not know what diseases he may have. You know that some infectious diseases can be transferred through contact with his sweat." The guard dropped Themba's hand like it was going to bite him. André capitalizing on this moment stepped forward and said,

"Here put these on, you can never be too careful" as he handed him a pair of gloves that he pulled out of his white lab coat.

The guard, a little shaken responded, "That's OK I will do it later" and then he dropped the keys into the pocket of his policeman uniform jacket and escorted the three of them out of the room. Trying to be casual, they awkwardly walked away. Each of the two guards picked one the girls and their eyes followed the rhythmic, almost hypotonic sway of their butts as they walked away down the corridor.

When they were out of sight from the guards, André broke away from the girls and went around the side of the building and headed for the side gate. The gate was a strong metal structure attached on both ends to a concrete wall. The wall was at least eight feet tall and had razor sharp barbed wire coiled along the fence line. André saw that the gate could only be opened from the inside, so he looked around for something he could use to keep the gate from closing. The gate had a spring tension that forced it to stay closed. André found a thick piece of tree branch which he dragged and placed at the door jam. This kept the door slightly ajar. Satisfied that this will work, André hurried back to the girls to prepare for the next step of this operation.

CHAPTER 37

Piet Coetzee sat in the side street outside James Anderson's house and scratched his head. Something was wrong here. James had not left his home in two days. The lights were on in his apartment and went off at the same time at night the day before. That was too much of a co-incidence. Piet was sure that the light was on a timer. So where is James and why hasn't he left his apartment for two days.

As Piet thought about James, his mind wondered towards André. Where was André? He knew that André was not at home, but how did he slip through his fingers? He wondered whether the two men were collaborating together. If he could prove that beyond all doubt it would boost his career and place him back in favor with Commander Villiers. His career and all that he worked for, went down the drain when the Commander called him an incompetent idiot. It was as if every one at the station had heard the Commander, for they were avoiding him now and he even believed that he had heard the men sniggering as he walked pass. If only he could bring down both James Anderson and André together in conspiracy, he would be a hero. Piet sat in the car and racked his brain on how he could manufacture evidence on these two men that would tie them together. He needed something that would standup under scrutiny and yes there will be scrutiny because of James's reputation in the media.

The more he thought about it the more convinced he became that he should start from the source, the Black mute in the hospital. Piet was not sure what he would find out but it was better than sitting here, doing nothing. He could drive to Durban and see the mute, maybe talk to the guards and try to gleam any tidbit of information that might give him a clue. The thought of doing something grew stronger in him until it exploded in his mind. He pounded the dashboard with his fist and said to himself,

"That's it. I have had enough. I am not going to take this lying down". With that he turned on the ignition and fired up the engine. He shifted the car into drive and headed for Durban to see Themba.

******

Themba held his breath as the guard walked into the room to fetch the Thermos flask. The guard looked briefly at Themba and satisfied that all was well; he grabbed the Thermos flask and headed out of the room. He heard the guards pour out two cups of coffee and settle down to enjoy their break. After a few minutes, Themba heard the one guard say,

"This coffee tastes different, I don't like it" and then Themba heard the splash of liquid on the ground. Themba figured that one of the guards threw out the coffee. Themba was hoping that he had drunk enough of the coffee and that it was enough to knock him out. All Themba could do is wait and see how this develops. The minutes dragged on and Themba found it more and more difficult to remain still.

André drove the dark blue Mercedes Benz slowly down the side street and parked opposite the side gate to the hospital. Sitting next to him was Norma, who seemed calm and in control. André was nervous and kept looking at his watch. Through his binoculars he watched the guards as they yawned and found it difficult to stay awake. André was not aware that the one guard had drunk only some of the coffee but because Meena used a potent sedative he had enough to also make him sleepy. Approximately at eight in the evening the guards were sprawled across the corridor, sleeping like babies.

André looked in his review mirror and saw the other car that was driven by Meena parked further up the street. Meena and Buhle drove in that car and were part of the backup plan. There were no other cars in the street. It was risky for either Meena or Buhle to ride in the car with André as that would raise suspicion should a police vehicle pass them. Having persons who were Non-white ride in the car with a White person was frowned upon and may be sufficient reason for the police to stop and inspect the car.

André pressed the steering pads twice emitting two short blasts from the car's hooter. It was ironical that the car was parked under a sign that had a picture of a car hooter with a line through it signaling that hooting in a hospital area was forbidden. After a few minutes André and Norma got out of the car and closed the car doors gently. The plan was for only André and Norma to fetch Themba. Meena and Buhle would watch the street. They will also signal using the car's hooter if a problem arises.

As André and Norma were getting ready to cross the street to the gate that André propped open, they saw a pair of headlights come up the street. They quickly hid behind a thick leafy shrub that served as a fence. The car came up the street and parked across the side gate in line with the dark blue Mercedes Benz. Piet Coetzee stepped out of the car and his eyes fell on the Mercedes Benz parked across him. It was an unusual sight as cars were frequently broken into at night and a luxury car like the Mercedes would be a temptation.

Piet walked to the car and peered inside. He spotted the car keys still in the ignition and he immediately became suspicious. As he reached for his gun that was holstered at his side, Norma emerged from the thick shrub noisily. As she straightened up she tugged at her panty waist band, making it seem that she was pulling up her panties. Her skirt was hacked up high and she rearranging her skirt to drop it back in place. As she did these maneuvers, she said in a giddy tone and slurred words,

"Where are your manners, son? You should turn around and look the other way when you see an old woman pee." With that she giggled and continued still adjusting her skirt.

"I had to go before I peed in my pants and I am too far away from home to wait. So I saw this quiet street and this shrub was a perfect spot". André grabbed a rock and was getting ready to charge Piet but he relaxed when he heard Piet say,

"Lady you should not be out here alone, it is dangerous, please get out of here before I arrest you and throw you in jail for loitering." André then heard Norma apologize,

"I am sorry officer" and scurried into the car and fumbled with the keys. Piet expressed an expletive in disgust and turned to leave for the side gate. With a few quick strides he reached the gate and immediately became alert and suspicious when he saw the tree branch used to prop the gate open. He immediately forgot about Norma as he opened the gate and raced towards the hospital wing which housed Themba. As he did he closed the gate behind him, leaving André and Norma stunned when they saw their lifeline to Themba cut.

CHAPTER 38

Themba heard the two short blasts from a car's hooter coming from the side street and he knew it was time. He quickly extracted the key from under his pillow and freed himself. He raced into the bathroom and changed into the clothing that André brought him. He put on the shirt and admired himself in the mirror. He never owned a new shirt before as he always wore hand me downs. The new shirt made him feel good and as he patted down the front of his shirt he felt good. He was ready to face the world.

Piet Coetzee came charging into the remote hospital wing corridor and screeched to a halt when he saw the two guards lying fast asleep on the floor. He went to the guard closest to him and kicked him viciously in the ribs to wake him. The guard who had a reduced amount of the sedative from drinking a few sips of coffee, grunted with pain as somewhere in his consciousness he felt his ribs fracture under the blow.

Piet drew his gun and rushed towards Themba's room kicking the door open as he charged in. Piet cursed when he found the bed empty and he became enraged. Someone was going to pay for this. The image of the open gate, the Mercedes Benz and the lady that emerged from the shrubs flooded his mind. He should have followed his gut instinct and arrested that woman. He had to get to his car and call this in. An all points bulletin on the car will help capture those suspects. Piet turned to leave and as he did he found himself face to face with Themba who had just exited the bathroom. Piet was stunned as he did not know that Themba was standing behind him. Piet took a moment to focus and then he sprung into action. As Piet raised his gun, Themba's forehead smashed into the bridge of his nose, and he heard the bone break. The sound of it exploded in his head and he reeled back becoming blinded with blood gushing from his nose.

The blow to his face stunned Piet and struggling to stay up, he grabbed at Themba's shirt for support. Piet's fingers hooked on to the shirt pocket and the shirt tore under his weight sending him sprawling to the floor. Piet tried to get up but a second blow from Themba to the side of his head dropped him like a stone, unconscious. Themba looked at his torn shirt and he grimaced. His new shirt did not last long. As he pulled at the shredded pieces of his shirt his eyes fell on Piet's police issue shirt, which was still intact. Without thinking about it, Themba undid the buttons on the front of the shirt and flipped Piet over on his face and stomach and proceed to remove his shirt. He put on Piet's shirt and patted it down. He felt complete again. The shirt was a little tight on him but Themba did not care, he did not want to go out into the street undressed. Themba smiled when he saw that Piet's pen was still in the shirt pocket and he patted it down. Finally he got the pen he was asking for several months ago.

Outside Themba's room, the one guard was struggling to wake himself from the sedation. The sedative was potent even though the guard had taken in a reduced quantity. Through a haze and falling in and out of consciousness the guard saw Themba leave the room. He removed his gun from the holster and tried to focus on the figure. Through cloudy and half closed eyes, all he could see were outlines of a police uniform and decided not to fire in case he shot his own colleague. Little did he know that the prisoner he was supposed to be guarding was the one wearing the police shirt.

André and Norma were panic stricken. They were so close to saving Themba and now they were helpless. They stood there, deciding on what to do next. They knew that they would be in danger very soon once Piet finds the unconscious guards. They also knew that they could not leave Themba who is also in as much danger if not more. As those thoughts racked their brains, a figure emerged from the gate and headed towards them. In the darkness of the street they could not make out the person but the police shirt was obvious. Both Norman and André stiffened as they considered their escape routes. André's heart lurched in his chest when he saw the dark figure emerge into the light and the familiar smiling face of Themba came towards him. André ran up to Themba and hugged him. Meena and Buhle drove down from their parking spot up the street and Buhle opened the door for Themba and hugged him as he got in. André said to Meena,

"Go quickly and we will see you at our agreed meeting place." Careful not to speed, Meena drove off with Themba safely in Buhle's arms crouched low in the back seat.

André got into their Mercedes Benz and Norma joined him, after scouting around and gathering a few objects. André was too hyped to ask her what she was up to, so he started the car and drove off in the opposite direction to Meena.

Piet shook his head to force himself awake. He staggered to the door just as he heard the Mercedes start up. He raced past the disorientated guard and kicked open the gate jamming it in the open position. As he reached the street he saw the Mercedes casually drive away. He ran to his car to give chase. He pulled open the car door and fell into the seat. He reached for the keys in the ignition and his hands fumbled for the key. It was not there. Piet was dead certain that he had left the keys in the ignition. Rage was clearing his mind and he focused. His next best option was to call for backup and have the Mercedes stopped. He reached for the radio mike and once again it was not there. The mike with its coiled connection was gone.

There was no time to waste. Piet saw that the guard had a radio on his belt. He bolted back to the hospital and found the guard still trying to shake his drowsiness. He bent down and reached for the guard's radio and as he did, the guard seeing a figure with a white undershirt, brought up his gun and pointed it at Piet. In the guards blurry and confused state all he saw a figure dressed in a white undershirt. Since the figure was quickly coming towards him he considered it a threat. The threat was more likely the prisoner trying to get his gun. The guard's glazed over eyes looked at Piet and fired two quick blasts at him. The first bullet hit Piet at the jaw bone and the bullet traveled across his lower jaw and disintegrated the lower jaw. The second bullet ripped through the side of his cheek across this tongue and left a messy hole on the other side of his face. Neither of the bullets were fatal but nevertheless they did a lot of damage to his jaw and mouth.

Piet spun around and collapsed on the guard pinning him down on the floor. The vanishing tail light of the Mercedes Benz in Piet's memory was the last thing he recalled as his mind plunged into darkness. The prisoner had escaped and there was nothing he could do about it now.

Norma sat in the front seat of the Mercedes Benz and giggled. She was having fun. Even when she confronted Piet in the street, she enjoyed the little diversion she had created. Now that she sat with Piet's car keys in her hand and his radio mike at her feet, she wondered what else she could do to make Piet's life miserable. She said aloud,

"This one is for you Misty"

CHAPTER 39

The peaceful sedate neighborhood of Berea, a suburb of Durban was shattered with shards of ambulance sirens and armored military vehicles. Inhabitants in the White only neighborhood peeked curiously through slits in their lace curtains at the commotion in the streets. Most of these folks have never seen an armored military vehicle and thought that they only existed in movies and television shows. It was no wonder that they feared for their lives and looked at their Black South African maids and gardeners through hateful glasses with lens forged from generations of ignorance.

Commander Villiers paced up and down the corridor barking orders into a two way radio. He was furious when he received the news that Themba had escaped. The commander was even more furious when he heard that Piet was at the hospital and that he was injured by one of the guards. News reported in the papers of this type of injuries hurt the reputation of his organization and the Commander needed to plug any news leaks. He pondered on this situation during his drive to St Andrews Hospital in Berea and needed to find a way to blame the injury on Themba. This would help his case against Themba when he is arrested. It would also go a long way to ensuring that a death sentence is handed down. He would charge Themba for the assault and murder of Johan in the sugar cane field and the brutal attack on Piet. He would also be able to demonstrate that Themba was part of a larger conspiracy. He could illustrate this by reporting that an underground movement had organized themselves to help Themba escape from a high security prison in a relatively short time. The Commander had decided that Themba had done him a favor for he could turn this around and use it against him.

Piet was taken to the hospital for emergency treatment to his face especially his lower jaw which was shattered by the bullets. The guards were given drugs to counteract the sedatives and they now sat cowering in the corner of the corridor waiting for their fates to be decided. Their careers were certainly ruined. They did not know who they hated more;

Themba for having caused all this or themselves for being outwitted by an unconscious mute.

Commander Villiers demanded the immediate capture of Themba and his accomplices. He gave descriptions of a White male and female and an Indian female and one Black female. The commander had expected that Themba's accomplices would try to get Themba out of the country as soon as possible. In his estimation they would head for the closest border and that would be the border between South Africa and Lesotho. The commander had a map of the area rolled out on the desk and he took a black marker and marked a cross at different border posts between South Africa and Lesotho. He turned to his Lieutenant and ordered,

"They will try to make it to the border at Sani Pass. They wouldn't try it at night as the road is treacherous and can only be maneuvered using a 4x4 vehicle. Take some men and head out to that border and wait for them. Kill them if they try to make a run for it"

The Commander knew that the Sani Pass was a treacherous pass through the Drakensburg Mountains. The pass was the only road from KwaZulu Natal to Lesotho. The path through the mountains was a series of steep narrow roads with hairpin bends that could only be negotiated with a 4x4 vehicle using three point turns. At night it would be dangerous. The South African border post was located at the foothill of the pass and one needed to go about five miles uphill through the mountains to the Lesotho border. Lesotho is a land locked country of approximately twelve thousand square miles located on the east of South Africa. This independence state is surrounded by South Africa and is a country that is a public supporter to end apartheid in South Africa

******

After leaving St Andrew's Hospital, all five of them drove to a house on the outskirts of the city where they had a chance to freshen up and map out a plan for the next step. They were planning to leave South Africa and seek the safety of Lesotho. The big challenge that they had in front of them was, how they would pass the South African border post. They did not realize that their challenge just got bigger with the Commander's orders to double the guards at the border post into Lesotho. Buhle and Themba spent some time alone to deal with the grief of losing the baby while the others planned their escape strategy. André and Themba communicated through signing and Themba described to André what had happened when he was confronted by Johan, the policeman in the sugar cane field. Emotions were high in the room as they discussed the "Harding massacre" and the events leading up the present.

If Norma could have heard the Commander give those instructions she would not be feeling as good as she did. Norma had a similar map rolled out on the kitchen table and pointing to the Sani Pass, she said,

"That's where we will pass into Lesotho and freedom from oppression." André looking concerned said,

"We cannot do that at night, it is impossible and only a 4x4 vehicle would make it through the mountains". Norma smiled and peeled back the curtain slightly. A Jeep 4x4 was parked in the rear of the house out of view from the street. André was about to ask how she managed to arrange that, but decided to let it go. He was getting a certain appreciation for her innovations. Norma looking at the group said,

"We need to go now as it will take us through the night to reach the border." With that Norma folded the map and they all prepared to leave for the Sani Pass. Norma was having fun and only shared what they needed to know on a need to know basis. She did this so that if any one of they were captured they would not give up the escape plans under torture. Norma got in as the driver and André as the co-pilot sat in the passenger front seat. Themba and Buhle lay in the rear of the vehicle covered with some blankets. They did this so that a policeman casually passing by will not be suspicious when he sees a White couple driving an expensive 4x4 vehicle at night with a Black couple sitting in the rear seat. The trip would take them about five to six hours on mainly highway roads until they reached the Drakensburg Mountains. Once they left the lights of Durban, they passed two major cites without any incidents. Norma made sure that she stayed just under the speed limit so as to not attract attention. Norma drove in silence as the tension mounted in the vehicle. Just before they arrived at the Sani Pass Norma pulled up at the town of Himeville and announced,

"We will change transportation here."

André was confused and was about to say something when Norma put her finger to her lips in a gesture to be silent. She pointed to an army vehicle parked a short distance at the local bar down the street. Norma quietly said,

"It looks like they are sending re-enforcements to the border post. We need to do something about that."

Norma thought for a moment and then quietly went to the Jeep's toolkit and extracted a pair of pliers. Summoning the others to be quiet she casually walked to the army vehicle and did a quick check to see where the occupants were. The street was deserted as it was early in the morning but she stayed in the dark shadows cast by the buildings. After she established that they were relaxing in the bar and stocking up with beer and other food items, she quickly ducked under the front of the vehicle and looked for the wires that went to the headlights. Being an army vehicle it sat higher off the ground so that it was easy for her to get to the wires and cut them. She then tucked the wires so that it was not obvious that they were cut. Accomplishing her task, she quickly walked back to the Jeep smiling to herself and said quietly,

"Another one for you Misty."

CHAPTER 40

André who was watching all of this with interest whispered as Norma got close to him,

"Why did you cut the headlight wires?" Norma smiled and said,

"Elementary my dear Watson, when the lights don't work the guard will think that it is a fuse and they will wait for daybreak to continue their journey to the border. The point is to delay them and not alarm them. If I cut the ignition wires or let the air out of their tires it would alarm them and they can summon for help. The non functioning lights will give them a reason for not driving through the mountains in the dark, a task that they were not looking forward to anyway." André smiled; he was really getting to appreciate this woman's ingenuity.

Norma led the three of them to the rear of the building. At the rear there was a shed that had three horses saddled and tethered to a post. A young Zulu boy sat close by and when he saw Norma he got up as if he was expecting her. Norma went up to him and spoke briefly to him in Zulu. She gave him several Rand notes and he thanked her and then disappeared down the side of the building. The other three of them just looked at each other quizzically and shrugged their shoulders in confusion. Norma explained the next phase of the plan and the three of them mounted the horses. Themba and Buhle were used to horses and were expert riders whilst André made a couple of attempts to mount the horse and eventually succeeded with Norma's help. Themba and Buhle stifled a smile as they rode along André who was wide eyed with apprehension. Norma followed them closely with the Jeep up the path leading to the Sani Pass.

Although it was almost daybreak, it was still dark when they arrived close to the South African border post at the bottom of the Sani Pass. It was time to execute the final stage of the escape plan. Norma went ahead with her Jeep, the sound of the engine alerting the two guards at the post. At this time in the morning the border post was closed and the guards were intrigued at the approaching vehicle. One guard stood outside the little office building guarding the boom gate with his rifle at the ready while the second guard sat behind the desk with his gun at the ready in its holster. The three horses and riders stopped out of view behind some trees close to the border post. The three riders stroked the horses to keep them calm. Norma stopped the Jeep and got out giggling and staggered towards the guard. The guard shone his flashlight at Norma and then inside the Jeep. When he saw that it was empty, he relaxed and let the rifle drop to his side.

Norma pretended to stumble and fell towards the guard. Amused he caught her and trying to be authoritative he said,

"What are you doing here, you are drunk". Norma smiled sweetly, hiccupped and then said,

"I got lost; I want to go to Himeville." Norma was getting good at this play acting. With every drunken maneuver she made she became more believable. The guard looking at this episode as entertainment to finish off his shift escorted her into the office. Once inside the office, Norma put on her best performance amusing the bored guards. Through her play acting Norma heard the rustling of the grass outside as the horses made their way around the boom gates. Norma picked up the rubber stamp and stamped her forehead and then shrieked with laughter. The guards couldn't help but laugh with her. Norma allowed some time to pass while she continued with her drunken antics. The three riders on their horses back made their way passed the border patrol into no man's land between South Africa and Lesotho on the treacherous Sani Pass. They quickly started their uphill climb on the Sani Pass to the Lesotho border post. This was a five mile climb to the top but the horses were sure footed and they obediently trudged on.

When Norma felt confident that the three of them were well on their way past the South African border post, she started to wind down. Daylight was also breaking and the guards were expecting to end their shift soon. Norma looking weary, asked,

"Which is the way to Himeville?"

The guards gave Norma directions and cautioned her to be careful. They looked at her as she left and the one guard looked at the other guard and put his finger to the side of his head and twirled it in a circle signing that she was crazy. Norma headed back to Himeville and as she passed the armored vehicle carrying the re-enforcements heading to the border post she waved. Little did they know that they were closing the stable doors after the horses had bolted.

The three riders rode for about five miles until they came to the Lesotho border. André was anxious as he was not sure what was going to happen next. All Norma had said was,

"There will be someone there to meet you, you will be safe."

When they arrived at the Lesotho border André's face broke into a very relieved smile when he saw James Anderson at the gate. When they reached the border, the three of them dismounted and each in turn hugged James. James excitedly said,

"I had negotiated with the Prime Minister of Lesotho to clear your entry into Lesotho. This government is very sympathetic with your cause to fight the oppression in South Africa and was willing to help."

James arranged for the horses to be watered and fed. The three of them walked to James's 4x4 vehicle and climbed in. James explained the next steps by saying,

"I have seats on the next international flight for the three of you to fly to England. The flight will leave out of Maseru which is the capital city of Lesotho. We will drive there directly from here." André looked at the weary travelers and said,

"Firstly we will stop at the resort here, where you can freshen up and get something to eat." James continued as he drove away,

"You will be given political asylum in England and you will be safe."

That day Themba, Buhle and André sat in the plane as it took off from Maseru for the long flight to England. This time André was in his element as he sat comfortably in his seat. André suppressed a smile as he watched Themba and Buhle squirm in their seats as the plane lifted off the ground. They had never flown before and held on to each other, drawing on each other's strength for their future life together. Themba ventured to look out of his window at the disappearing landscape below and he thanked the spirits for keeping him alive to be part of these experiences. He looked at Buhle and knew that it was going to be his mission in life to make her happy. Buhle feeling Themba's gaze on her also had similar thoughts and they both looked at André and thanked God for making him a part of their life.

CHAPTER 41

The sound of the dialysis machine was almost hypnotic as it passed the blood through cleansing filters and back to his body. Nina had become accustomed to that sound as she sat almost every week for the last five years watching Devraj undergo the cleansing of his blood. Nina looked out the window of the hospital ward at St Mary's Hospital and found that the dark cloudy afternoon sky reflected her mood and her life, all sixteen years of it. Nina could remember the day that Devraj was diagnosed with renal disease and he and Rupin were discussing the prognosis. She remembered looking at Devraj and then at her dad, Rupin and asking him,

"You can fix Uncle Devraj can't you? Can't you make him better?"

The both of them looked at her and Devraj was the first to react, he picked her up in his arms and gently kissed her on the cheek and said,

"It will be OK, I will get better" and that made her feel better. Her dad just sat there, his face showing no emotion. That was the way it had always been for as long as she could remember. Her Dad, Rupin, was never cruel to her; he gave her whatever she needed. The one thing she wanted from him and never received was his emotions. He never showed any emotion towards her and was always aloof. Through the sixteen years of her growing up, she could never engage him in emotional conflict and she had tried. When all else had failed she tried to make him angry on several occasions but he would just concede and walk away. She always felt that he was too afraid to hurt her as she did not belong to him. It was obvious that she was not his child biologically as she knew that she was adopted. What really seemed to puzzle her was that she did not really resemble the Indian people in her appearance. In fact as she grew older her appearance had started to change and she looked more like a descendant of the Zulu nation then that of an Indian. Her skin tone darkened and her hair became very curly almost frizzy. Her Mom, Sheila had spent a lot of time trying to straighten her hair in the mornings especially on school days. Nina remembered that it hurt as her mom had pulled her hair so tight into a pony tail that it pulled the skin on her forehead and made her very uncomfortable. Nina had never complained as she knew that her Mom was doing that so that her hair did not look so different to the other girls in her all Indian school.

Nina remembered with some bitterness that she was constantly the target of many racial jokes and innuendos as the school girls had constantly picked on her saying that she was in the wrong school. Nina recalled that she could bear the brunt of this abuse on her appearance for she would be the envy of all the girls in the afternoon when her Uncle Devraj would come to fetch her to escort her home after school. Devraj for his age was very good looking and single and many of the girls had secretly adored him and were envious of her relationship with him. No other girl in that school had any parent or relative come to the school in the afternoon and escort them home and she felt special. Since the school was located in the vicinity of the neighborhood all the girls walked alone after school to their respective homes.

A tear rolled down her cheek as she looked at Devraj now, he was so weak and fragile and the thought of losing him weighed heavily on her. Although both her parents had taken good care of her, they did not show much emotion towards her. They loved and cared for her as one would love and care for a neighbor's child in their custody. Nina felt guilty even thinking about this as her parents had provided very well for her. She was not lacking for any material possessions and they were always attentive to her every needs, but the closeness was not there. She hoped on many occasions that they would lash out at her in anger and show some passion, but they never did. She craved attention from her parents even if it was negative attention.

Even when her mom, Sheila was on her death bed, dying of ovarian cancer, she showed little emotion. She would lie in bed and look at the wall. Her dad would sit with her mom every day when he came home from work and he would just sit there not saying a word. It was Devraj who stopped by almost every day and spent time with her and helped her with her homework and did things with her. Nina didn't know how she would have managed without him. It was about the same time that Nina's mom, Sheila passed on, succumbing to the effects of the cancerous disease when Devraj was diagnosed with renal failure. Nina's mind went back to that time and she swallowed nervously. It was five years ago but the emotions she felt at that time still haunted her to this date.

Her dad, Rupin grew even further apart from her as he withdrew into a shell. Nina turned to Devraj for emotional support and guidance and Devraj devoted his life to her. And now here she was; the only person she was close to was slowly fading away. Nina's eyes filled with tears as she looked at Devraj; someone who has given her so much and who means the world to her. How could she go on without him? Devraj had never made her feel like she was different, but she knew that she did not belong. Nina decided that when Devraj was done with this week's dialysis treatment she was going to approach him to help her locate her real parents.

The night before she had gone into her dad's study and found him as usual reading a medical journal. Nina waited to be acknowledged and when Rupin looked up at her through the top of his glasses, she said,

"Dad there is something I want to talk to you about. It is a sensitive subject, but I really need to do this."

Her Dad said curiously,

"What is it, Nina?"

"Dad, I want to find my biological parents", she blurted out. Her Dad looked at Nina for a long time and slowly removed his reading glasses and set it down on the table. Her Dad spoke slowly,

"Nina, do you really want to know who your biological Mom and Dad are?"

Before she lost the courage to do so, Nina quickly said,

"Yes Dad, I want to know". Rupin drew in a breath and slowly exhaled. He said quietly,

"You should ask Devraj who your parents are; he can tell you."

Having said that, Rupin put on his reading glasses and proceeded to read his medical journal. Nina was amazed how quickly she felt alone, a stranger in her own home. As she turned to leave she reflected on how odd her Dad's response was to her request. She hadn't expected him to help her with this quest but thought it only fair to ask him first. She should have gone to Devraj in the first place. She was fairly confident that if there was anyone who could find her real parents, it would be Devraj.

As Nina turned and left Rupin in his study, she pondered on the odd way that Rupin responded to her request. "Ask Devraj who your parents are; he can tell you." Nina asked almost aloud, "Dad thinks that Devraj knows who my parents are, does he know?"

CHAPTER 42

The South African Truth and Reconciliation Commission (TRC) was set up by the Government of National Unity in 1995 to help deal with the politically motivated transgressions that occurred during the apartheid years. Perpetrators of the politically motivated transgression could also give testimony and request amnesty from prosecution. Amnesty however was not guaranteed and only a small percentage seeking amnesty was granted it. The country was reborn with its conception celebrating the release of Nelson Mandela from captivity on Robben Island. The subsequent years were pregnant with change in a country poised to give birth to a single nation for all ethnic groups. The general elections in which all South Africans were given a vote promised to deliver South Africa into a free country for the once oppressed Non-white population. The TRC played an important part of healing for the country and many re-lived the horrors of the apartheid years. One of the cases the commission had on its agenda was the Harding Massacre and subsequently hearings were scheduled. Now sixteen years after the massacre, researchers working for the Head of the Investigative Unit collaborated with James Anderson to locate key witnesses and survivors of the massacre. James had contacted Themba who at the time was living in London. Themba, Buhle and André had made their home in England after been granted political asylum in the country. Themba agreed to travel to South Africa to be present at the hearing.

It was sixteen years ago when the massacre had occurred but Themba remembered it as if it was yesterday. In the privacy of his thoughts Themba played through the events of that night in the sugar cane field and his encounter with the police. He anguished over the death of the baby and held himself responsible for her death as he had failed to protect her. He carried the burden of guilt and pain alone; he did not want to burden Buhle with additional trauma from those memories. Now the time had come for him to face his demons.

The pilot on the South African Airways 747 Jet announced that they were preparing to land at Jan Smuts Airport in Johannesburg, South Africa. Buhle looked out the little window in the plane with some apprehension. Memories of the "Harding Massacre" came flooding back her. For the past sixteen years while she had lived in London she had not allowed herself to dwell on that massacre and the loss of so many lives, including her baby. Being so far away had helped, but now that she was back in the country, it was very difficult for her to separate herself from that tragedy.

Buhle looked over at Themba and admired his calm spirit. He was a stabilizing force in her life and it gave her strength to endure the torment she felt in her dreams. Not a day had passed when she not longed to see her baby and hold her close to her. She would have given anything to just to get one more look at her baby. She had hoped that as time passed, the pain would go away but it did not. She did not have closure and in her mind she could not accept that the baby had perished. It might have been easier for her to get the closure she needed if she had seen the baby's burial. She endured her pain alone and did not share it with Themba as she felt that she would inflict even more guilt on him for not protecting the baby. She knew that Themba carried that guilt inside of him and she did not want him to suffer anymore than he had done. Themba was the best thing that had happened to her and she loved him dearly.

She recalled the day that he went in for his Laryngeal transplantation operation. The surgical operation to replace his larynx was totally successful and after a year of speech therapy Themba was able to speak. His voice was like music to her ears. Themba had so much to share with her that they would sit for hours and talk. He had waited until he could talk to propose to her because he wanted to say "I DO" at the altar and he wanted everyone to hear it. André was the best man at the wedding ceremony. André and Themba had become very close friends and were inseparable. Themba's artistic skills were highly valued and many commercial art agencies offered him working assignments. The three of them lived comfortable lives and were grateful to have left the country safely when they did.

The TRC held its hearings in Cape Town and the three of them traveled there by plane from Johannesburg. Cape Town was located at the southern tip of South Africa. Norma, Meena Ansari and James Anderson flew from Durban and met them in Cape Town. The reunion was emotional and the six of them spent that evening re-living the painful events that brought them together. Whenever the memories dragged them down a dark hole, Norma came to the group's rescue with hilarious remembrances of the way they had tricked the guards. Norma and Meena Ansari explained how they had later set up a safe house to care for and support unmarried pregnant women and abused women. Meena found that her caring spirit helped to run the safe house while Norma lobbied for support from political groups that were anxious to show the voting public that they cared.

The next morning André, Themba and Buhle attended the hearings. The court room was crowded and a sense of anticipation hung heavily on the room. The crowd in the court room gasped when Piet Coetzee walked in and slowly made his way to the witness box. His face was disfigured with his bottom jaw totally disfigured. It was obvious that some restoration work was done to his face but the injury was obvious. He carried a small mechanical device which he pressed against his larynx when he needed to talk.

With much difficulty and labored breath, Piet recounted the events that led up to the "Harding Massacre". When he talked about Johan and Themba's shooting Themba sucked in a breath and sat attentively, his heart pounding in his chest. Buhle reached for his hands and held it in hers tightly. Piet admitted that Johan had died as a result of a struggle and he was shot in self defense. Piet admitted that Johan was a loose cannon and it was obvious that Themba acted in self defense when Johan was shot. Themba exhaled, realizing that he was holding his breath. He felt a huge weight lift off his shoulders and a tear welled up in eyes. Themba sat riveted to his seat as Piet was questioned about the baby. He was afraid of how Buhle would handle the news of the baby's tragic demise.

When questioned about the baby, all Piet could say was that he thought the baby was killed in the struggle as the blanket the baby was wrapped in was full of blood. Piet went on to say that he thought the baby was taken away for the mass burial. Buhle struggled to keep her composure and openly cried on Themba's shoulder. Piet also stated that there was a witness to the incident. Piet said that he saw a black man who had turned and ran away from the scene and it was for that reason that Piet gave chase. He stated that this man had run towards the village, so he called in the riot squad to assist. Piet then went on to say that the riot squad went into the village and panicked when several Zulu men emerged from the shadows. Piet bowed his head as he stated that this triggered an unfortunate series of events that led to the massacre of the inhabitants of the village.

Piet bowed his head several times during this confession for the weight of the whole incident weighed heavily on him for many years. Tears openly ran down his cheek as he talked about the killing of so many villagers. Piet talked about the surveillance of James Anderson the reporter and Andre Pretorius, who they suspected was Themba's accomplice, but they now know that they were mistaken. When Piet admitted to poisoning Andre's dog, Themba had to restrain Andre from jumping over the railing and choking Piet. Themba's calm presence did a lot to restrain Andre, and Buhle was thankful for that; this was not the place for revenge. That day in court was emotionally draining for both Themba and Buhle and they were thankful to get away from that courtroom and all the memories that it dredged up.

The six of them went out that evening to a restaurant for dinner. It was not a celebration as there were too much of tragedy uncovered during the trial, but they needed to be together to honor the friendship that developed between them. It was a testament that people of all races could co-exist regardless of their skin color. Governments and organizations that propagated the separation across racial lines only served to cultivate hatred for each other. During dinner Themba presented a framed sketch to the "girls" Norma, Meena, James, aka Jean and Buhle. The sketch beautifully done by Themba using pastels was a picture of four girls, a pregnant Buhle, Meena, Norma and Jean, the alter ego of James Anderson. Themba stood up and took a sip of water and then cleared his throat, and eloquently said,

"Ladies, I salute you for your bravery, courage and determination." As he said that Themba raised his right hand to his forehead in salute. Themba continued,

"You are viewed as the weaker sex, but true strength does not come from outward brute force, it comes from within. You all have demonstrated that. You took on the dreaded Security Branch of the South African Security Forces and won. You ladies have true strength. Even James, who through the guise of a woman, was able to overcome his hurdles. I am privileged to be in your company. I salute the women in our lives." Saying that Themba looked at André and they both saluted. That was a fitting end to a very tiring day and they parted company for the night.

That evening at the hotel Buhle was very preoccupied and so was Themba. Buhle needed to have closure and decided that when they flew back to Durban the next morning she would visit the village mass grave and lay some flowers for her baby. She also decided that while she was in the area she would visit Annie DuPlessis, the farmer's wife, who had been so kind to her during her employment and more especially during her pregnancy. Buhle also needed do this by herself and talked to Themba about this. He was very understanding and said that he would wait for her at the hotel.

The next morning they all flew back to Durban and once they checked into their hotel, Buhle looked at Themba and said softly,

"I know that Piet Coetzee said that my baby was killed during the struggle, but deep inside of me I feel that she is alive". Themba held her tightly and whispered,

"It is OK to keep her alive in your thoughts", but before he could complete his sentence, Buhle pulling apart from him said firmly,

"No, she is alive, I can feel it. I can almost hear her calling out for me. I have to go to the village one more time". Themba looked at her, concerned for her emotional state of mind. He made a mental note to seek counseling for her when they returned to London. Themba knew that the trauma of yesterday's court hearing must have been more than she could bear. He wanted to take her away from all of this and return to London. Little did Themba know that fate was about to turn his world upside down.

CHAPTER 43

Nina was looking at Devraj while he was dozing during his weekly dialysis treatment. She was depressed as she watched him become weaker by the day over the last few months. His only hope was to have a kidney transplant but there were no donors that matched his DNA. She was going to ask him to help her find her biological parents, but she had not summoned the courage to do so. She felt that she might hurt his feelings if she asked him and that may ruin their relationship. She decided that she was going to approach him today after his treatment and this made her nervous. Her throat was dry from her anguish and she decided to go down to the hospital cafeteria and get something to drink.

Annie DuPlessis was sitting with her husband Kurt DuPlessis in the cafeteria at St Mary's Hospital. Annie had accompanied her husband to St Mary's Hospital for his regular medical check up. Annie and Kurt had decided to retire and move to a retirement home on the South Coast of KwaZulu. The sugar cane farm was not doing as well and the DuPlessis's decided to sell it and retire. They had spent many evenings reminiscing about the good times they had on the farm and the people who had worked with them. They remembered Buhle and still thought fondly of her. Whenever Annie thought of Buhle she would draw a white cotton hanky from her pocket and wipe a tear from her eyes. It was a tragic day when she read in the paper that the villagers had been killed in a fight with the riot squad. She knew that Buhle lived at that village and since she had not heard from her since that awful night, she concluded that Buhle had also perished in that massacre.

Annie had left the space in the utility room that Buhle had used unchanged over the years, and to this day she was not sure why. She felt that Buhle's presence was always there and ever since Buhle had left, Annie had not found a replacement. She had become very attached to Buhle especially during the pregnancy. Annie never got over Buhle's tragic demise. Annie was talking to Kurt when she stopped in mid sentence. Her eyes bulged with disbelief. Kurt looked at his wife with concern. She sat there, her mouth open in mid sentence and her eyes were fixed on the young girl that just walked in looking for the vending machine. Kurt said trying to break her trance,

"What is it Annie, have you seen a ghost?" Annie gasped and without taking her eyes of the young girl that just walked in, she whispered,

"I think I am seeing one now" and with that she got up and went over to Nina who was studying the choice of drinks in the vending machine. As Annie approached Nina she said,

"Oh my! You look just like your mother; you are a spitting image of her, except for your eyes". Annie was not known for subtleties but she was gentle and it came out in the tone of her voice. Nina turned to face her, somewhat surprised but intrigued. Now standing face to face with Nina, Annie could see Buhle's round face and pleasant smile. Even the way she tilted her head inquiringly reminded Annie of Buhle. And then realizing that she had not introduced herself, Annie apologized for her rudeness and said with genuine concern,

"Buhle, your mother, worked for me, even while she was pregnant with you and we absolutely loved her. We were horrified to hear of what happened to her, we are truly sorry." Annie realized that she had rambled on without giving the poor child a chance to talk, so after mentally calculating the number of years that had passed she asked,

"Let's see, you must be at least sixteen years old?" Nina was overwhelmed and was dumb struck for a moment so she just nodded. Nina looked at this lady with kind, soft eyes, and tried to piece together what she had just heard. The words that kept surfacing in her head were "You look just like your mother". With her heart pounding and her pulse quickening, Nina tried to stifle her eagerness to know more, she asked as calmly as she could manage,

"Did you know my mother?" As if that was so obvious, Annie replied with a smile,

"Yes my dear, she used to work for me until that tragic day when so many perished". Nina was now completed intrigued, her emotions swirling between sadness and excitement for having found someone who knew her biological mother. She proceeded with the questioning,

"Can you tell me about my mother?" before Annie could respond Nina fired a barrage of questions about her mother. Annie held up her hands in a gesture to stop Nina and then offered to the excited Nina,

"Dear if you want to know more about your mother, then come to my farm house, and I can tell you all about her over a cup of tea".

We still have some of her personal possessions and you can see the room in which she sometimes stayed overnight". Annie then went back to her handbag that sat on the table with Kurt and pulled out a small piece of paper and a pen and wrote down her address and directions for Nina to come visit. She gave Nina the paper and hugged her while her bemused husband watched.

Nina bounded up the stairs two at a time to get to Devraj. She was so excited that she did not even get her drink and she couldn't wait to tell Devraj all about her meeting with Annie DuPlessis. She raced into the room but Devraj was still napping. Nina paced the floor trying to contain her excitement. Finally she decided that she would head out to the DuPlessis residence and talk to Annie. It was already late afternoon and it would take her at least an hour or two to get there. She would have to take a taxi to the Zulu village and then walk to the DuPlessis residence. She was so intent of finding out who her mother was that Nina did not consider the danger she was placing herself in by going alone in the taxi and walking through the sugar cane fields. The taxis were small closed vehicles that carried about eight people, but in most instances the taxi operators filled them to capacity and then stuffed in a few more passengers. A sixteen year old girl alone in this general area was at great risk.

Nina couldn't wait any longer she wanted to find out more information about her mother, she was impetuous she wanted to do it now. She sat down on the bed next to Devraj and wrote him a note. The note read,

"Dear Uncle Devraj, I know who my mother is and I am going to go talk to Annie DuPlessis about her. Annie is the lady who employed my mother and knows all about her."

Nina then wrote down the address of the DuPlessis residence. She then left an additional message which said,

"I will tell you all about it when I see you this evening. I will take a taxi to get there as it is too far to walk, but don't worry about me I will be safe." Nina then left the note on the bedside table for Devraj to see. As she was about to leave the room she went back to the bedside table and scribbled on the note "I love you, uncle Devraj" and then went over to him and gently kissed him on the forehead.

Nina virtually sprinted to the taxi stand and grabbed the first taxi heading out to the Zulu village. She got there safely although several young men eyed her with curiosity and salivated with fantasies that they played through their head as they watched her. Once she got off at the village she again sprinted towards the DuPlessis residence anxious to talk to Annie.

CHAPTER 44

Annie was surprised to see her so soon but was pleased to see her and greeted her warmly. She led her to the patio and offered her a cup of tea and some biscuits. They sat on the porch for about an hour and Annie told her everything she knew about Buhle. Annie had to stop and couple of times to dry her eyes and blow her nose as she recalled the events that led to the day of the massacre. Annie mentioned Themba on several occasions as being Nina's father but as she did that Annie in the privacy of her thoughts struggled to see any likeness of Themba in Nina. Annie looked at Nina and said,

"Let me show you where Buhle sometimes stayed over for the night. She did that when ever the weather was bad."

Nina was preoccupied as she tried to digest all the information she heard from Annie. Somewhat numb with emotion, Nina followed Annie to the utility room. The small makeshift bed still sat in one corner of the room and Nina was saddened to see the simple structure that used to be her mothers bed. Annie put her hand on Nina's shoulder and asked,

"Nina, would you like me to leave you here alone for awhile?" Nina nodded and appreciated the opportunity for privacy to grapple with her turbulent mind. She lay down on the makeshift bed and closed her eyes and tried to imagine her mother's presence. She was saddened to know that her mother was dead, and wished that she had a chance to know her.

As Nina lay on the bed, she noticed the secret hiding place that Buhle had carved out in the crawl space. From her vantage point she noticed a cloth bundle stashed in the corner of the crawl space. Nina reached over and carefully extracted the bundle and her heart raced as she opened the ties. The bundled contained various hand drawn sketches and a small journal. Nina sat up on the bed and peeled the drawings one at a time. She was struck at the great detail of each sketch and although they were done with a pencil the sketches had a life like detail to them. Each sketch was signed "yours forever, Themba". Nina had heard mention of Themba's name from Annie DuPlessis as being her mother's boyfriend and Annie presumed that Themba was her father. Even as she asked herself "is Themba my father?" Nina knew in the heart that he was not. For some reason she felt that Themba was very special to her mother but he was not the father to the child her mother carried. Nina paused for a moment and thought about it. Who then was her father?

Nina continued to page through the sketches and her heart almost stopped when she saw a sketch of Buhle. Nina knew immediately that the sketch was that of her mother since it resembled herself closely. It was like looking in a mirror at an older version of her self. Nina held up the sketch and gently kissed it and then held it close to her chest and softly said "I love you mommy". Nina had developed a deep relationship with Devraj, but she had craved a relationship with a mother figure, a woman to woman relationship. She was at an age that she needed a female figure in her life. Sheila was more an acquaintance than a mother and since she passed on, Nina did not have a female figure in her life.

There were more drawings and sketches and they all were very good. It was obvious to Nina that Themba had loved Buhle very much as the drawings depicted that. At the bottom of the drawings Nina found the journal. Excitement rose in Nina as she saw that the journal was well used and had several pages of hand written text. Nina turned to the first page to read but her excitement was interrupted by Annie DuPlessis, who walked in and asked,

"Are you done, dear, do you need more time?" Nina closed the journal and looked up at Annie.

"May I keep these?" Nina asked pointing to the sketches and journal.

"Yes, my dear you may, they now are all yours" Annie replied cheerfully.

Nina could not wait to get back on the road so that she could read the journal in privacy. Nina left the farm and thanked Annie DuPlessis for her kindness. Daylight was fading and she decided to take the shortcut through the sugar cane field to get to the taxi stand. Nina could not contain her curiosity any longer and opened up the journal and started reading as she walked. She had to stop a few times to re-read what she had just read as each word burrowed deeper and deeper into her soul. Buhle had talked about Themba and Mapoza and the Zulu village. Nina was intrigued as she read about her mother life.

She was half way through the shortcut through the sugar cane field when she came across the Buhle's account of what happened in the sugar cane field on that fateful night sixteen years ago. It was that tragic night that Buhle was sexually attacked by Devraj. Buhle described in detail the events of that night, but she did not mention any names in her account. She however described the passenger in the car and as Nina read on it was becoming obvious to her that she was referring to Rupin. The description of the birthmark on his face and his general appearance was a giveaway clue. Buhle then went on to describe the man that chased her down and sexually attacked her and once again the description fitted Devraj, her uncle Devraj. Nina had to re-read this several times and each time reaffirmed the previous read. The words swirled in her head as it was becoming painfully obvious to her that her uncle Devraj had raped her mother and she was the product of that terrible evening. Realizing that she was conceived by an act of violence and not of love, Nina felt dirty. She unconsciously wiped down the front of her blouse with her hands and shivered with disgust. A conflicting emotion racked her confused emotional state as she thought of the person, Devraj. He was kind and thoughtful and always had her interests at heart. She adored him and looked up to him; she could not see him as a rapist. She grappled with the thought that Devraj her biological father was also her mother's sexual predator. Nina closed her eyes in an effort to block out reality, a technique that always worked for her as she grew up.

******

Meanwhile back at the hospital, Rupin walked into Devraj's room looking for Nina. When he got to the room, Devraj stirred and opened his eyes. Rupin asked,

"Where is Nina?" Devraj was still groggy from his nap and the dialysis and he looked around the room. He shook is head in confusion saying,

"I don't know; she was here before I fell off to sleep" Rupin looked around for signs of her purse or other personal effects that may give them a clue as to where she had gone. Rupin saw the note on the bedside table and read it out aloud. There was stunned silence in the room. And then it dawned on them that Nina was in an unsafe area especially since she was planning to take those taxis to the DuPlessis residence. Although

Devraj was weak he jumped out of bed and grabbed his car keys, saying to Rupin,

"I am going to find her". Rupin who was always slow to react was now spurred into action. He quickly said,

"I will go with you" and they both hurried out to Devraj's car. In order to save some time they decided to take the short cut through the sugar cane field to the DuPlessis farm.

Nina was startled out of her shocked state when she saw this vehicle hurdling towards her in the cloud of dust. Devraj saw Nina standing on the side of the road and he sighed with relief. At least she was safe. Devraj braked to a halt skidding along the loose gravel. The car came to a complete stop close to her. He rolled down the window and was about to say,

"Thank goodness you are OK" when he saw the expression on her face. Their eyes met, each searching for an answer. The air was charged with energy. Devraj sensed that something was wrong but he could not figure out what that was. Nina looked at Devraj her emotions scrambled, she was angry and lost; she was disillusioned; she was sad. She wanted the ground to open up and swallow her. Rupin looked at the both of them and sat there not knowing what to do. Being Rupin he did what he did best and that was nothing; as he did, that night, sixteen years ago. Devraj was the first to react, he got out of the car to talk to Nina, but she turned clutching the journal and bolted into the sugar cane field, like her mother did sixteen years ago. She ran scared, away from her predator holding on to her treasure.

The door chime that came on when Devraj opened the door jolted Rupin into action and for the first time, he realized he could not just be a bystander. He had a responsibility.

While all this was going on, Buhle was driving her rental car on her way to visit Annie DuPlessis. She was running late so she decided to take the shortcut through the sugar cane field. From a distance she saw some commotion down the road and her heart leaped for it brought back memories of that fateful night. Memories came flooding back to her of the injustice that was done to her and she froze. She sat in the car for a moment and watched a little girl being pursued by an Indian man. Anger built inside of her and her stomach twisted in sheer rage. History was repeating itself and she was not going to sit and let that happen to someone else.

She got out of the car and ran through the sugar cane field towards the girl. Nina came charging through the sugar cane stalks and crashed into Buhle who grabbed her and held her protectively. Devraj, weak with his disease, was winded and fell to the ground. Rupin came charging through the sugar cane stalks and screeched to a halt when he came across Buhle and Nina. The air was stagnant with apprehension. Buhle like a trapped animal glared at Rupin ready to tear his heart out. And then a glimmer of recognition crossed her face. Buhle remembered this face; it was not one that injected fear into her. Rupin looked at Buhle and thought he was seeing double, for he was seeing Nina all grown up. Nina had not yet looked to see who had stopped her. She broke free and ran to Rupin crying,

"Daddy, Daddy". Buhle saw Nina's face for the first time and froze; it was like looking in the mirror. Her gasp caused Nina to turn around and look at Buhle. Nina was stunned; she was looking at the person in the sketch, Buhle, her mother.

All three were silent, for words could not describe what each was thinking. And then as if choreographed Buhle pointed to Rupin, Nina pointed to Buhle and Rupin pointed to Buhle and they said in unison,

"It's you!" Devraj's feeble cries as he passed into unconsciousness broke the stalemate that developed and it was Nina, who cried out,

"Uncle Devraj" and ran to him. She kneeled down and held up his head and sobbed,

"Daddy, please don't leave me". Buhle walked to where Devraj lay on the ground and the recognition was instantaneous. She recoiled as the memory from sixteen years ago hit her. Rupin who normally was dormant took charge of the situation. He faced Buhle and said,

"A terrible injustice was done to you sixteen years ago, but a beautiful child was born. Let me take Devraj to the hospital and once he is attended to we can talk. I will explain everything". Buhle barely heard Rupin as she was still in shock. She looked at Nina and her heart swelled with love; tears rolled down her cheek. Buhle held out her hands to Nina, who ran into them and they hugged.

CHAPTER 45

Nina stood and watched Devraj as he labored to breathe. The heart monitor flat lined for a brief moment and Nina held her breath, waiting for the heart monitor to ping again. It was an agonizing few seconds until the monitor signal spluttered and a regular ping filled the room. Nina twitched and slowly exhaled. Buhle stood behind Nina and held her tightly, feeling her tender body tremble. Buhle was deep in her thoughts as she also watched Devraj fight for every breath. It was not in her nature to hate anyone and although she was violated by the man now struggling to stay alive, she could not hate him. She felt that his evil transgressions early in his life had come to claim him now. He had served his time in this lifetime in different ways. He was the key figure who located Themba when Themba was in the custody of the Security Branch. He took over guardianship for Nina when her adoptive parents couldn't provide parental love. He had no life of his own, and lived looking for salvation from his friend. Buhle felt that a more powerful divine presence had administered justice for Devraj.

When they returned from the sugar cane field, Devraj was taken into intensive care and while the doctors worked on him, Rupin, Buhle and Nina went to Rupin's office to piece together this tragic puzzle. Buhle made a call to Themba and left a message for him. Her message simply said,

"Themba, please come to St Mary's Hospital when you get this message. Don't worry I am OK and I have good news to share with you. I cannot tell over the phone, you have to see this for yourself."

Rupin sat behind his desk nervously fingering a large brown envelope on his desk. Nina sat on the edge of her seat opposite the desk, kicking her legs aimlessly, her mind preoccupied and emotionally confused. Sitting next to Nina, her one hand protectively holding Nina across the shoulders was Buhle. She demonstrated an inner strength that matched her posture. She sat erect and her presence dominated this office. Rupin keeping his eyes on the brown envelope said softly,

"You already know some of the details, so let me start by saying that Devraj is Nina's biological father. I have the DNA test results here in this brown envelope." Rupin looked up anticipating some response but got none. The fatherhood was a foregone conclusion. Rupin continued,

Rupin explained how he got to adopt Nina and how the system had tracked her as Indian, thereby losing the traceability. Buhle listened with interest, while Nina twirled her hair and continued to kick her legs. She had shut off a long time ago; the only thing on her mind at this moment was that Devraj was dying and the presence of her mother sitting next to her. She would sneak a look at Buhle every now and again, wondering what kind of person she was.

Nina found that she had tuned Rupin and his explanations off since Devraj was on her mind and she was worried about him. She asked if she could be excused as she wanted to go to the intensive care unit to sit at Devraj's bedside for a while. It was there that Buhle caught up with her and both mother and daughter watched Devraj as he fought to take in every breath. After some time had past Buhle excused herself from Nina so that she could go and meet Themba at the Hospital reception area when he arrived. Nina preferred to stay with Devraj. Rupin in his typical manner continued to make his rounds at the hospital and stayed busy. He was saddened at Devraj's condition but dared not show it to the world. He dealt with it internally and resigned himself to the fact that he would face life alone.

The flat line signal on the heart monitor triggered off an alarm at the nurse's station and several hospital personnel and doctors came charging through to Devraj's bedside. Amidst all the orders that were shouted out by the Doctors the flat line tone persisted and Nina was ushered out of the intensive care unit. Nina knew that Devraj was not coming back to her and for an instant, she heard his cheerful voice calling out her name, but it was gone before she picked up her head.

Nina walked slowly to her favorite spot at the hospital. It was the garden attached to the cafeteria outdoor dining area. She and Devraj spent many lunch times there when ever she came to the hospital to see him. Rupin would join them occasionally, but his visit was a courtesy and he always had some emergency and had not stayed long. Nina played back the events of this day. She found her real dad, and then found her real mom and then lost her real dad. She wondered how much more she could handle. Nina was heart broken, she loved Devraj and now he was gone. She wanted to find her real mother and now she had, but why did she feel so cheated and empty. Nina sat there for a while and wondered if she was being punished for wanting more in her life than she had. She had a comfortable life with Rupin as her Dad and she had a friend in Devraj.

Nina was sitting on the steps leading to the garden, feeling depressed and she wondered what her life will be like without Devraj. From the corner of her eyes she saw an orange object roll towards her. The object was a small orange fruit and it rolled up to her and gently bumped her leg. She looked up to see where the fruit came from and she spotted a middle-aged Zulu man sitting at the table drawing on a sketch pad. He did not acknowledge her presence or give any indication that he had rolled the orange towards her. His face was pleasant and he had kind eyes. Nina was curious as to what he was sketching, so she got up and went towards him. When she approached him he still did not acknowledge her presence but turned the sketch book slightly towards her, his gesture inviting her to take a look at the drawing.

Nina smiled when she saw the sketch as it was a sketch of her with the garden as the backdrop. The man had already finished the sketch of her and had started on a second figure. The second figure that he was drawing was of a man standing behind her. Nina stood and watched the man draw the second figure. As he drew the face, tears rolled down Nina's cheeks for the realization hit her. The man was drawing the face of Devraj from a small photograph he kept hidden on his lap. Nina had seen that photograph on Devraj's desk many times. Tears overwhelmed her as she also realized who the man was. Nina looked at his gentle face and put her arms around the man she knew to be Themba.

The End